I0664171

Fairhaven's Legacy

...the adventure continues...

M. Geoffrey Clough

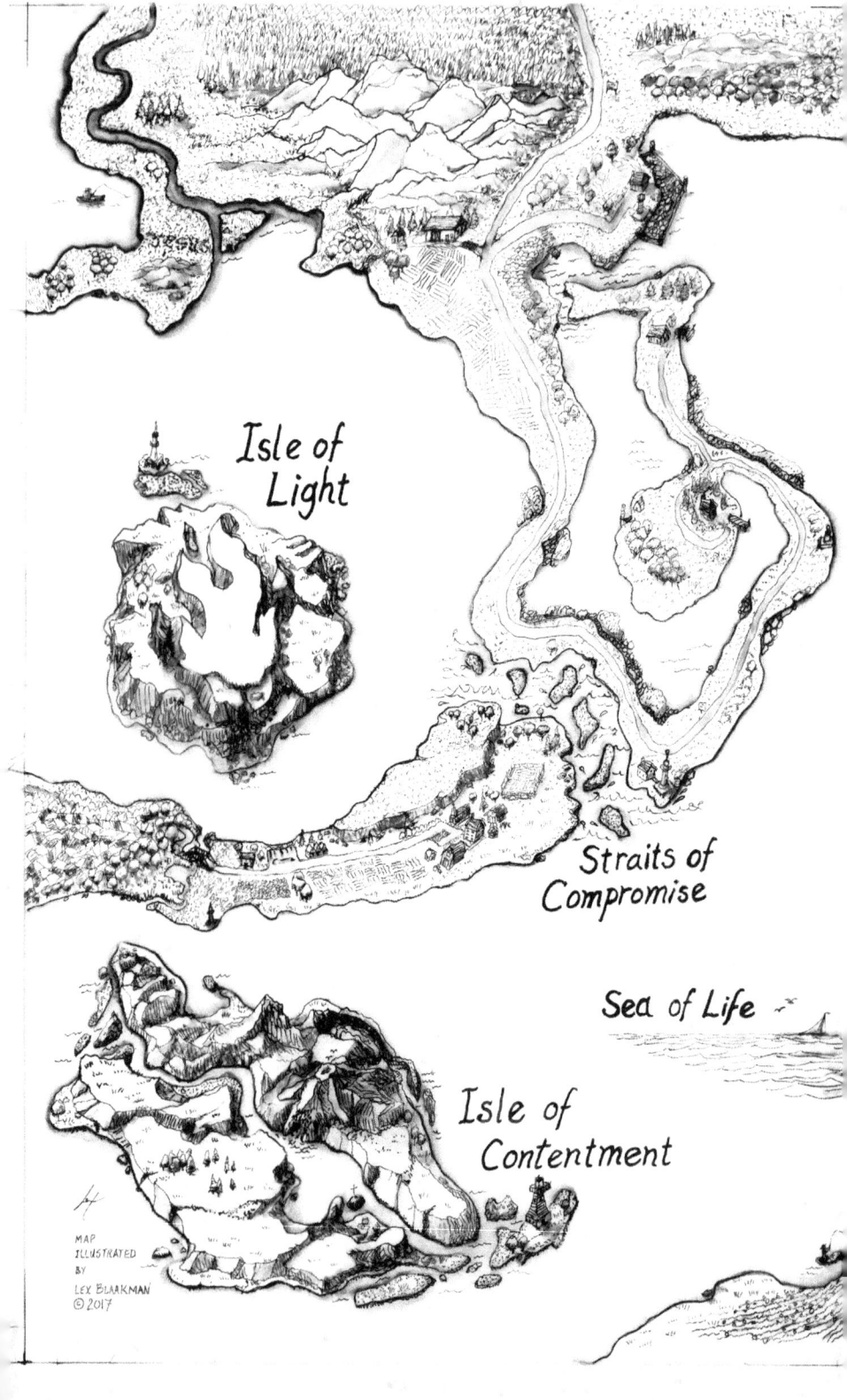

Isle of
Light

Straits of
Compromise

Sea of Life

Isle of
Contentment

MAP
ILLUSTRATED
BY
LEX BLAAKMAN
© 2017

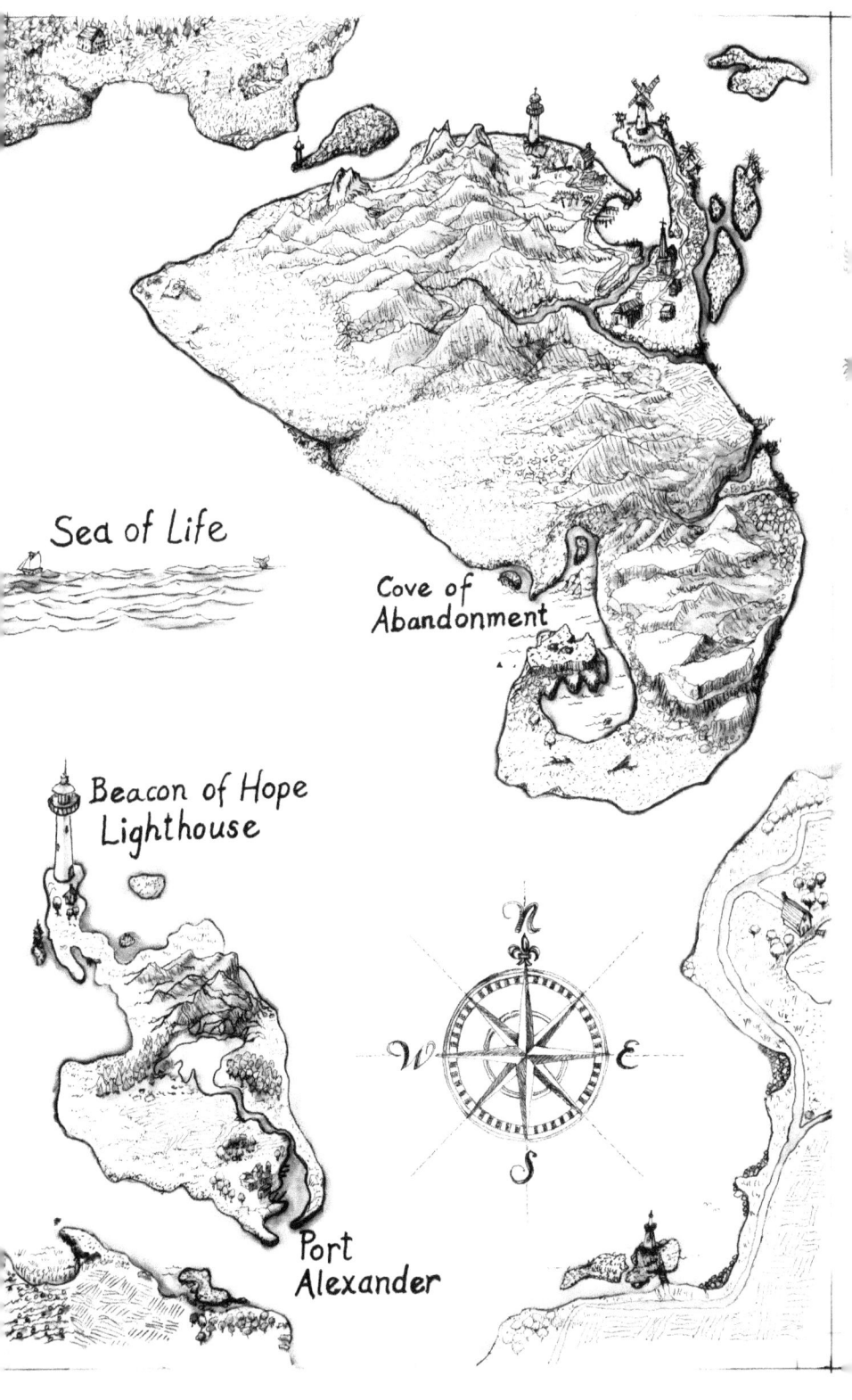

Sea of Life

Cove of
Abandonment

Beacon of Hope
Lighthouse

Port
Alexander

FAIRHAVEN'S LEGACY:

... the adventure continues...

M. Geoffrey Clough

IISBN: 978-1-945423-49-9

Copyright © 2023 M. Geoffrey Clough

All rights reserved. No part of this publication may be reproduced, distributed, or transmitted in any form or by any means, including photocopying, recording, or other electronic or mechanical methods, without the prior written permission of the publisher, except in the case of brief quotations embodied in critical reviews and certain other noncommercial uses permitted by copyright law. For permission requests, write to the publisher, addressed "Attention: Permissions Coordinator," at the address below.

Five Stones Publishing (ILN)

Permissions Manager:

Randy2905@gmail.com

www.ilncenter.com

Printed in the United States of America

Cover Artist Deborah Wester
Map Illustrator: Lex Blaakman
Editor: Mary Pratt
Publisher : 5 Stones Publishing (Randall E. Johnson Director)

Fairhaven's Legacy

In the first book: Fairhaven: Adventures On a Sea Called Life: A young ship named Fairhaven had been sailing on the Sea of Life for years, searching for acceptance, family and purpose. Along his journeys he met a number of characters who became his family of friends.

In Fairhaven's Legacy we find Fairhaven's family of friends has set out to restore a friendship lost long ago, with one who believed a lie that led to a dark and lonely path.

It's time he knew the truth. The key lay in the word: Forgiveness.

Not only asking for it and receiving it, but also conquering the battle within: how to forgive himself.

Cast of Characters:

Fairhaven - A young adventurous ship

Blanding - A grandfatherly tugboat

Seaworthy – An orphaned seagull

Alby (fondly known as Uncle Alby) – The seagull who raised Seaworthy

Salty - A teenaged cat. She and Schraeder are best friends.

Schraeder - A young stowaway mouse.

Shelby - A one clawed hermit crab. Wears glasses. Very proper.

Crow who later becomes known as **Karl** - Went to flight school with Seaworthy. Got caught up with a bad group.

Cutter - Leader of the Deceiving ships. Was destroyed by the Navigator in first book.

Copper - A ruthless ship. Cutter's number 2 in command. Also destroyed by the Navigator.

Professor Watt - An owl, he runs the Beacon of Hope Lighthouse.

Brave and Faithful - A rowboat. Formerly known as Fearful-and-Doubtful.

Brickwater - A galleon ship, tormented by Cutter and his Deceiving ships.

Lovely - A beautiful swan struggling with an imperfection.

Gwendolyn and Walter - A fun-loving walrus couple.

Chloe - A butterfly with a unique gift.

The Navigator - A true and fearless friend to all.

DEDICATION

A friend and I met at Tim Hortons to catch up. I told him about publishing my first book: Fairhaven. Adventures on a Sea called Life.

He looked at me and said, "You've got to write a sequel."

Sadly he died a few weeks later.

That's when the sequel began to emerge. So this book is dedicated to my good friend Bob Campbell.

You are greatly missed.

ACKNOWLEDGMENTS:

Special thanks to my readers who have enjoyed the adventures of Fairhaven and his family of friends...

...and to my family and friends who have helped me bring this story to life.

Chapter 1

A Longing for Blanding

The excitement at the Beacon of Hope Lighthouse had quieted after Fairhaven and the Navigator had departed.

"Marvelous lunch, Professor," said Schraeder as he pushed back his soup bowl, wiping the fresh bread crumbs from his face with his sleeve.

"Ahhh..., try this." Professor Watt shook out a cloth napkin and handed it to him.

"That works," smiled Schraeder.

"Sure does, it's purrrfect," said Salty with a grin, revealing her own need for one.

"I knew you were going to say that." Schraeder rolled his eyes in frustration as the Professor began to hand a napkin to Salty.

"What's this for?" grumped Salty.

The Professor tapped his chin with his wing and raised his eyebrows. What had been a peaceful moment had now begun to descend into the usual bickering.

"Not again," the Professor said as he adjusted his glasses and massaged his chin in disbelief. "I thought we had worked through all this."

Salty and Schraeder began to quiet down, and each replied as they'd been taught by the Professor, to accept each other's differences and to be kind and respectful to one another.

"Sorry, Professor. I've got to work harder on my reactions to what I imagine to be criticisms when it's really just non-judgmental fun," said Schraeder.

"Me, too," Salty said with a sly smile, "Still thought it was purrrdy good."

The Professor wiped his face with his napkin, and went outside to the deck overlooking the Sea of Life.

"I'm coming with you," said Schraeder, leaving Salty alone.

"What did I do?" Salty questioned, looking around the empty room.

Schraeder caught up with the Professor as Salty hustled to join them. She could see her friend was not enjoying their usual 'tit-for-tat' banter, and added "What's wrong?"

"I miss him," Schraeder sighed.

"Who?"

"Blanding."

Silence...

"Me too," came Salty's soft reply.

"He was kind of gruff but I liked him anyway."

"What about Fairhaven?"

"I miss him too, but he's with the Navigator. But Blanding is left ... alone." They stood there silently, watching and listening to the soothing waves splashing ever so slightly against the lighthouse foundation.

The Professor, noticing the uneasy hush between the two friends, wrapped his wings around them, comforting them like a doting grandpa. "Don't worry. The Navigator loves Blanding and he'll watch over him."

Chapter 2

Back Home

"The island looks great," said Seaworthy as they approached Alby's home.

"Yeah, it's nice to be back," Alby added.

"It will be even nicer once I'm on dry land and not being bounced around like a beach ball in perpetual motion," said Shelby, quite weary from the journey from the Beacon of Hope Lighthouse.

They flew past the waterfall and saw the sunken remains of one of Cutter's ships still blocking the channel to the hidden cove. They flew through the hanging vines which gently tickled their sides, causing them to laugh, then... 'Plop!' They had dropped Shelby into the drink.

"Oops!" Seaworthy smirked.

"Oh, he'll be alright," chuckled Alby.

After landing on the shore, they relaxed, stretching out in the sand while waiting for Shelby. In the thick silence, they surveyed the area, taking in its beauty.

"Look, there's the spot where Shelby rescued Fairhaven, when he butted that rocky walled section. He was very brave," recalled Seaworthy.

"Yes, he was. He certainly is tougher than he appears."

Memories of Fairhaven cascaded over them, bringing smiles and tears. Weary from the flight, they fell asleep.

Slowly but steadily Shelby made his way under water, complaining all the way, muttering to himself: "'We're your friends'. Sure you are, dropping me like that."

Shelby quieted down, coughing out the water that flooded his home during his unexpected splashdown into the sea. He kept crawling to his favorite beach spot. As he drew closer, he recognized the familiar underwater terrain and began singing a joyful little song, anticipating the warmth of the sun:

"I'm a happy little crustacean, I am, I am...

hmm, hmm hmm, hmm, hmm.

I'm so happy to be back home again."

He snapped his claw to a clever syncopated rhythm. He paused... and grinned. "I like that," he said to himself. He snapped his claw again. Then continued:

"I'm as free as a bird, tra, la, la, la, la..."

"Wait a minute, a bird?" Then his countenance soured. "Why, those two birds dropped me in this water. When I get my hands on them…oooooh!" he sighed. "There I go again. My claw, oh, never mind, Shelby," he said to himself. "They really are my friends. I should forgive them and move on with our friendship. Yep, that's what I'm going to do."

Arriving at the beach, he found Alby and Seaworthy asleep. Bending down, he lowered his claw as if to pinch their webbed feet, then he hesitated, wondering if he should play a trick to even up the score. But when he noticed the sunlight filling the place and felt its warmth, it interrupted his thoughts. He decided to give up the revenge idea and enjoy his sunny little haven of rest.

Exiting his shell, he crawled to the warm sand, "Ahh," he softly exclaimed, nestling into a comfortable position. With one more brief sigh, he fell asleep.

"Do you think he thought we were sleeping?" Seaworthy whispered.

"Zzzz" snored Alby, completely unaware.

CHAPTER 3

REALITY SETS IN

Meanwhile Crow awakened to a cold and desolate wasteland, an apt description of his home at the Cove of Abandonment. Lonely, defeated, friendless and despondent, he sat on a branch of a decaying but still stately oak tree, staring at the sea.

"The Sea of Life, Ha! Life stinks!" he yelled to no one.

A cold, wet wind blew up, enhancing the dismal outlook. The breeze swelled the waves, casting annoying water droplets over his already chilled body. They dropped off his beak, but he gave no response. His inner brokenness and turmoil were too deep. His brokenness lay heavy on his burdened soul.

He began walking around the shoreline with his wings tucked behind his back, looking like a scientist calculating his options, while occasionally kicking a shell or a stick.

Crow saw a large boulder on the beach. Upon reaching it, he leaned on it and sighed so deeply that words could not express the emotion. When he opened his eyes, he began to stare into a small still pool of water. Sadness began to overwhelm him again. His face in the reflection seemed to say harassingly: "It's over. The Navigator will never forgive you. Who could ever forgive you for what you did to Brickwater? You're a crow and that's all you'll ever be."

SPLASH! A pebble entered the water and distorted his reflection in the water. Slowly the ripples worked their way to the edge and vanished, revealing his face and a figure standing behind him...the Navigator.

"Of course I forgive you," said the Navigator, "and I have already done so. I heard you the first time you called out to me, asking for forgiveness for your careless words. Remember? I told you it wasn't your fault that Brickwater perished. That was his own doing. The memory of Cutter is rekindling the thought that it was your fault when it was not. You need to speak to that hounding voice and tell it to leave. Then get up and walk away. That voice is a liar."

Crow looked back at his reflection with tears in his eyes and turned to ask a question. The Navigator was gone. Then Crow heard a quiet voice saying: "I'm going to send you a special friend to prove to you that I love you and forgive you."

Chapter 4

Shelby's Upgrade

Seaworthy walked over to Shelby while Alby slept. "Shelby," he whispered.

"Ah, what do you want now? Can't you see I'm sleeping and working on my tan?"

Puzzled, Seaworthy asked, "How can you talk when you're sleeping?"

Shelby raised up, put on his glasses and squinted. "What do you want, anyway?" shaking the sand off his back.

"I wonder what Salty and Schraeder are up to. I want to go back and see them."

"We've only been home a short time, and you want to go back already? My stomach is still doing somersaults."

"I think it might be a good idea to stop by for a visit," said Alby, yawning and stretching his wings.

"Well, that's fine for you two birds, but I'm staying right here." Shelby laid back down, took off his glasses and snapped his claw a couple times as a sign of retaliation for waking him up.

"That's fine," said Alby. "We'll tell them you say 'hello', ok?"

"Yup! Seaworthy, move a little to the left, will you? You're blocking the sun."

"Oops."

"Thanks."

Seaworthy and Alby walked away, chatting about when they would leave. They agreed they'd leave in the morning.

"Seaworthy, come with me. I want to make Shelby a satchel, a carrying type of basket to make his flights with us more comfortable." As they flew off to survey Alby's island home, they came across some palm trees. "Let's get some of these branches down to the ground."

Seaworthy broke off a few large ones, and then Alby began peeling the palm strips to weave them together. After a while Alby asked, "Ah, what do you think?"

"Looks pretty good to me."

"Tomorrow we'll check it out with Shelby. I think he will find it much more to his 'satisfaction', as he would say." They both chuckled as they flew back, carrying the basket between them, sure that Shelby would change his mind and return with them.

CHAPTER 5

A SECOND CHANCE

Salty and Schraeder woke up in the morning to a spectacular sunrise. Professor Watt was still enjoying a few zzzzs. The two went outside to enjoy the view. A breeze brought an early chill inside, for they hadn't closed the door.

"Good morning," yawned the Professor, the chilly air waking him. "Should we make some cocoa and then watch the view?"

"Sure," they both agreed.

The Professor thought to himself, "Ah, they finally agreed on something. This is going to be a good day."

As they headed inside, they heard a familiar voice yelling: "Coming in for a landing!"

It was Seaworthy and Alby carrying Shelby in the basket.

Then 'PLOP!" Down came Shelby, who was a little woozy from the flight. He landed on the deck and would have rolled over the edge, if it weren't for Seaworthy quickly putting his foot on top of his shell.

"That's quite enough of that. Kindly get your stinky foot off my home. Thank you," grumped Shelby, a little miffed at his entrance.

Everyone was glad to see each other. Hugs went around over and over again. Occasionally Shelby got stepped on, but he didn't say a word.

"Come on in, everyone; we're just about to make cocoa. Please join us," the Professor invited.

Seaworthy closed the door, and they all sat at the breakfast table. A slight but persistent tapping could be heard on the glass door. It was Shelby, locked out. He just stood and waved his claw. Salty let him in and gave him a boost onto the table, and Salty rejoined the ongoing conversation. Shelby began to complain but no one was listening; they were all busy talking amongst themselves.

Each one still missed Fairhaven, and many a tale was recited about adventures they each had with him. Blanding's whereabouts were also discussed, but Seaworthy abruptly interrupted the gathering to bring up a different topic.

"Guys!"

"Ahem!" said Salty, tapping her paws up and down on the table top.

"Lady and gentlemen," Seaworthy started again.

"That works," said Salty matter-of-factly, with a smile.

"Recently, I've been thinking about Crow. I wonder where he is and if he's ok."

"He's probably living alone back at the Cove of Abandonment," said Alby.

"What should you care? What should we care?" said Salty with an attitude that was echoed by others. "After the way he treated you in flight school and with his pal Cutter. Good riddance, I say."

"Well," started Seaworthy, "that was a while ago and Cutter's forever out of the picture. Maybe Crow's changed."

"Well, maybe not!" snapped Schraeder, out of character.

"I'm willing to start afresh. He was a lot of fun back at school in the beginning," Seaworthy added.

Salty and Schraeder each entered their own reasons for not showing any compassion toward Crow. Even Shelby began to side with them.

Then Professor Watt spoke up: "Maybe he does need a second chance, maybe he needs a friend. A true friend, like you are to each other."

Alby agreed with the Professor. "You can never have too many friends. We are indeed all friends here, but we also recognize that we are not purrfect. No pun intended, Salty."

Salty dropped her head onto the table with a thud, implying it was a bad pun for sure.

Alby continued: "You know we all need friends; we are very fortunate to have each other. Let's think for a moment. What would the Navigator do?"

Everyone grew quiet.

Seaworthy replied: "He'd give him a second chance."

"Well, I don't know if I'm ready to do that yet," sighed Salty, disparagingly.

"Salty, you and Schraeder argue a lot and yet you two make amends and are still friends. Wouldn't you miss him if he left and never came back because of what you said or how you behaved?" Professor Watt pointed out.

"Yes, I would," Salty replied slowly.

"Me too," echoed Schraeder.

"In the war of words, nobody wins," added Alby.

"Shelby, what do you think?" asked the Professor.

"Zzzz!" He was sound asleep in his comfy home.

"I think we should try to find Crow and reach out a hand of friendship," said Seaworthy.

Alby spoke up, "I can see this is not going to be an easy decision. Let's think about it over the next week and get back together."

"But I don't want to wait that long, what if he really needs a friend right now?"

"Patience, Seaworthy, patience." Professor Watt gently patted him on the shoulder.

CHAPTER 6

SEAWORTHY TAKES ACTION

After a couple hours Alby and Shelby were ready to go back home.

"Where's Seaworthy?" Shelby asked.

"I don't know, haven't seen him in a while," said Salty.

"Last time I saw him, he was walking around the property," Schraeder remembered.

Everyone looked all over the island and in every room of the lighthouse. No Seaworthy.

"You don't think he went off on his own to find Crow, do you?" hesitantly asked Salty, fearing she had driven him to that decision.

Alby spoke, "He must have. He was very determined to help him. Which is noble, but sometimes a rash decision can lead to an unexpected outcome."

Professor Watt mentioned; "That means he's possibly gone to the Cove of Abandonment. That's Cutter's old hideout. It's still a dark and desolate place."

"Hop in, or whatever you do," Alby said to Shelby. "Climb aboard your transportation basket."

"What's that?" asked Schraeder.

"It's a woven basket of palm branches, I coated it with some sap from one of the trees on my island. It helps the basket to stay afloat if we stop to rest on the water. It holds Shelby safely and there'll be no sudden drops." Alby looked at Shelby who looked unbelievingly back at him. "Well, it's supposed to do that."

"I will say it is comfy." Shelby scrunched down into his shell. "I'm ready for lift off!"

"Ok, I'm ready too; let's go. Is anybody else coming with us?"

Professor Watt couldn't go because he had to run the lighthouse. Ships depended on his readiness and the light to alert incoming vessels of danger. Salty and Schraeder couldn't fly, so they would remain behind with the Professor. Understandably saddened, the two wished them luck.

As they flew away, Professor Watt said "Let's ask the Navigator to grant them success, for they don't know what lies ahead."

"Navigator, wherever you are, you were there for us when we needed you, and we know you will be there for our friends."

"...and for Crow," softly added Salty. They each sighed at the end of the Professor's prayer.

"Shelby, we'll need to rest at home first and then leave in the morning. I don't want to fly tonight, there won't be a full moon," said Alby.

"You're the driver."

CHAPTER 7

HATCHING A PLAN

A surprise awaited them upon arriving home. They found Seaworthy pacing back and forth on the beach, trying to think of a plan.

"Seaworthy, you're all right!" Alby hugged his nephew.

"Everyone was worried about you. We thought you left to find Crow by yourself," said Shelby with concern.

"You were worried about me?"

"I must admit, I certainly was. You may be bothersome sometimes, but I do enjoy your company."

"Thanks, I just needed to be by myself. I can't think of any way to approach him. Maybe he'll refuse my company, or maybe he's..."

"Whoa, Seaworthy! You're thinking way too fast," said Alby.

"Yeah, you're always in such a hurry," added Shelby.

"Slow down, relax. Let's work this through together," said Alby.

"We've got to help Crow. If he turns us away, at least we tried."

"Let's sleep on it tonight and discuss our plans further in the morning," Alby recommended.

It was still a few hours before sunset and Alby watched Seaworthy continue trudging up and down the shoreline.

"Any ideas, Shelby?" asked Alby.

"I think the first thing is to get to the Cove of Abandonment. Then we could split up and search the island for Crow."

"I think that's the plan we should follow. Simple, yet it's a start," agreed Alby. Calling to Seaworthy, "I'm going to bed; see you in the morning."

Alby did not tell Seaworthy the plan so he wouldn't get all anxious and unable to sleep. Alby knew that it may be a harder adventure than they had ever taken before, and sleep may not be as pleasant there as it is at home.

CHAPTER 8

A STRANGE FLYING MACHINE

Back at the Beacon of Hope Lighthouse, Professor Watt settled in for the night. Salty and Schraeder stayed awake, listening to the ocean's waves.

"Think he's ok?" Salty asked.

"Yeah, it's Seaworthy. He knows his way around." A pause, then Schraeder added, "At least, I hope so."

In the morning Salty and Schraeder rose before the Professor. They began to explore the lighthouse grounds. They wanted to see if there were any secrets to discover. Professor Watt had given them permission to make themselves at home ever since the Navigator had them remain at the lighthouse with him, and he took great delight in each of them.

As they wandered, they discussed how they could help Seaworthy.

"What can we do? We can't fly. Fairhaven's gone. We're stuck here," Salty stated.

"No, we're not stuck here. The Navigator sent us here and he must have a purpose in mind," Schraeder responded. "Let's not give up hope. You never can tell what could happen if we keep thinking up ideas."

As they walked around, they observed a strange bunch of intertwined trees and bushes. As they approached it, they found a large shed. They pushed aside some of the shrubbery and discovered a door. Grabbing the door handle, Salty found it to be frozen tight, encrusted with accumulated salt from years of the ocean air blowing over it.

"Put some elbow grease into it, Salty," said Schraeder.

She determinedly gave it another try to get it open. As she struggled, Schraeder jumped off a branch and yelled: "Watch out! Coming down!" He landed feet first on the door handle. 'SNAP!' the handle broke off.

His effort flung him to the ground with the door handle landing right beside him. He picked it up and said: "At least we got it to move," smiling in embarrassment.

"Yeah, but will it open?" asked Salty.

They looked at the door and saw that it had opened a little but not all the way. They grabbed the edge of the door and pulled as hard as they could. Suddenly, a squeak, and then the door moved ever so slightly but just enough for Schraeder to squeeze in.

A voice behind them spoke softly, even jovially. "You two sure know how to open a door." It was Professor Watt. He had heard the snapping of the door handle and the commotion in the shed. "You know, this door hasn't been used in years."

"We figured that out," said Salty.

"You upset?" asked Schraeder.

"No, not at all. I've been wanting to get that door opened for years, though by the looks of it, I still won't be able to ease in there," holding his small pot belly. "You could have gone over here instead." Professor Watt pulled back some branches from a few overgrown cedar bushes, revealing a hidden door at the back of the shed.

"A secret door!" exclaimed Salty and Schraeder, surprised.

Professor Watt opened that door easily. They walked inside and peered through the cobwebs decorating the interior as if they were leftover streamers from a long ago party. Salty and Schraeder went past the Professor, who was standing there, memories flooding through his mind. As he looked, he spied certain objects that harkened back to long ago times.

Salty and Schraeder were quietly whispering, part in fear and part in curiosity.

Professor Watt noticed and bellowed: "You don't have to be quiet in here!" startling them. They turned and bumped into each other, while the Professor enjoyed a good laugh.

They began inspecting more objects, some leaning against the walls and uncovering items long in need of a good dusting. They found the shed to be about 20' wide and surprisingly 60' long with a sagging roof. They continued to brush away cobwebs with an old whisk broom they had found. Thankfully the sun was shining in through the dingy windows, revealing hidden surprises all around.

"This is like finding buried treasure," said Salty.

"Yeah," Schraeder agreed.

"Ah, now, there is nothing here of any treasure, just long lasting memories of my life here at the Beacon of Hope Lighthouse. Some fifty years now."

They continued to rummage through grimy old boxes, finding unique oddities here and there, when they stumbled upon an old faded plaque. Schraeder rubbed his arm over the nameplate, reading: 'Keeper of the Light: Walt Watt.' Salty and Schraeder stared in amazement.

"It's my graduation plaque," stated the Professor, taking it from Schraeder and adjusting his glasses to read the inscription. "This is from my studies to be a lighthouse keeper."

Schraeder asked: "Is it hard to be a lighthouse keeper?"

"Well, it takes time and preparation," Professor Watt answered. "But, it's a life I totally enjoy."

As the Professor admired his plaque, Salty and Schraeder continued searching and discovered an antiquated wooden door with stained glass windows and the door handle broken off, leaning against a wall.

Schraeder saw the handle next to the door and watched as the Professor bent down and picked it up.

"Ah, this was one attempt I made at getting the door open a long time ago. Um... kind of like the way you did today." He wiped his glasses and grinned at them. They all shared a good laugh.

Behind the door Salty and Schraeder found a weird looking contraption. They moved stuff out of the way and dragged it outside to get a better look. "What is this?" they asked.

"Oh, my, I've forgotten all about this." The Professor chuckled.

It was bigger than both of them had thought. They walked around it in amazement as the salty sea air blew away the dust. They scrutinized every little detail. Such a strange thing they had never seen before.

"It's a hang glider," Professor Watt explained. He started to piece it together and straightened out the canvas wing. He was smiling and chuckling to himself, remembering his earlier days when he had flown with it. He began mentioning times he and Alby would take it for some fun, catching some strong winds from the Sea of Life.

"Teach us how to use it," said Schraeder.

"This can make us fly?" asked Salty.

"Yes, it can."

A few hours later the hang glider was ready for testing, after the Professor had given clear instructions on how to operate it. He gave a few dry runs, showing how to walk with it and how to catch a thermal. Then he went back into the shed and emerged with two helmets.

"You'll need to wear these to be safe if you're going to mess around with this," he said while cleaning them off. "Ah

Choo!" He sneezed, knocking off his glasses. "It's been a while since they've seen any sunlight."

Surprisingly, the helmets fit quite well, though Schraeder needed some padding in his, otherwise it would have drooped down over his eyes.

A few days later after practicing under the supervision of the Professor, he said, "You both are doing very well. I've got an idea." He went into the shed and brought out something he had secretly been working on to surprise his two young friends. "Voila!" He grinned ear to ear, proud of what he was displaying. "This piece right here makes the hang glider capable of carrying both of you at the same time."

"Whoa! Too cool!" they both shouted.

After working together for a few more days, they began to formulate a plan to help rescue Crow. One day they tried out the hang glider without the Professor knowing.

"Are you sure we're ready for this?" Salty hesitantly asked.

"Let's go. No looking back," replied Schraeder with determination.

"One... two... three!" Off they ran down the slope heading toward the sea. As they reached the end of the cliff, an updraft caught them by surprise and lifted them high above the lighthouse within seconds. They had made it. They caught a thermal that carried them even higher and faster than they had imagined.

Fearfully they began yelling: "Professor Watt! Help us! Hurry, Professor Watt! Help us!"

The Professor was awakened from his afternoon nap when he heard their screams. He looked and could only faintly make out it was Salty and Schraeder clinging onto the hang glider.

"I'm coming!" he yelled, but to no avail; they were too far away to hear him. The Professor launched into the sky, flying as fast as he could. "Hang on!"

As the Professor drew closer, the winds grew stronger and put them further and further out of reach. In a last ditch effort to communicate with them, he put his wings over his mouth like a megaphone and yelled, "I'm sorry - I can't help you. Remember the Navigator." His voice faded, quickly drowned out by the wind's howl. He sadly turned around and headed back.

They couldn't hear the Professor. They were on their own. The sudden danger made them realize that to survive, they would have to work together.

"Are we heading in the right direction?" asked Schraeder.

"I remember going this way when we left Alby's with Fairhaven," answered Salty. "This is pretty cool," she added, "but a little scary too."

"Look! I think that's Alby's place," said Schraeder.

"Yeah, I think you're right," agreed Salty, "and they've probably already left to search for Crow's place. We've got to keep going."

Strong gusts came and went with no seeming effect on the hang glider, though they were growing tired.

"This takes more energy than I thought it would," observed Salty.

Some time went by when Schraeder exclaimed, "Salty! Look to the right!"

CHAPTER 9

FORGIVEN

C row had begun writing his own guilty verdict in the sand daily as a continual reminder of his shame and undeserved forgiveness, although by each morning the waves had washed away each entry. The beach had become like a brand new slate, a new leaf of tablet paper ready to be written on.

"I'm so sorry, Navigator. Please forgive me. I didn't mean for Brickwater to die because of my words."

The Navigator invisibly whispered: "I have forgiven you. I have sent the waves to keep washing away your etchings as a reminder of my forgiveness given to you."

Crow bent down and grabbed a shell to write it all over again, but this time he longingly cast his eyes up to the sky and asked: "Is it true?"

"Yes, it is," came the sense with the breeze.

He sighed and wrote again his own sentence of guilt. As he stood back to read his words, a soft caressing wave washed over his feet, surprising him. He looked down, thinking his words were washed away, but instead found a few scattered letters still legible. They spelled out:

'I .... f...org...ive....yo....u.'

The Navigator had once again reminded Crow that he loved him and forgave him. Tears fell like raindrops dripping off spring flowers in full bloom. He fell to his knees, truly feeling for the first time, "I'm forgiven. I'm free."

Laughter broke from the depths of his being. "I'm forgiven! I feel clean!"

CHAPTER 10

A NEW FRIEND ARRIVES

Crow flew from the beach, landing on his favorite branch in the old oak tree. As he sat and mulled over the current changes, he observed a chubby caterpillar making her way up the tree. She was humming and singing as she slowly approached him. Crow continued watching this happy little creature crawling toward him. Then she stopped and gave him a curious look, shrugged and stretched each of her 16 tiny legs. Then, shaking her fuzzy fur, she crawled upside down under Crow's branch and continued her happy humming.

"What are you so happy about?" he asked sarcastically. Crow had fallen back into the throes of his misery.

She paused, still upside down, and said: "I was born to fly." She kept walking and humming her little melody. Then she crawled on top of the branch and sat next to him.

Crow responded mockingly: "Are you serious? Do you really think you're going to fly? Ha! That'll be the day." Crow almost fell off his perch, laughing so hard. "Who told you that you could fly?"

"The Navigator told me."

Crow grew silent and turned away, subdued, thinking to himself 'Would the Navigator really forgive me?' He was remembering his earlier encounter. "How do you know him?" he asked.

"I saw Him rowing in a rowboat." Her memory returned vividly, recalling the incident word-for-word:

The Navigator said, "Hi, how are you?"

"Oh, I'm fine, just a little lost right now." I called out as I observed this man in glowing white, who had stopped beside me.

"I'm the Navigator and this is..."

He was interrupted by: "Brave-and-Faithful, that's my name. See, my name is on my oars. Brave, Faithful" showing her his engraved names.

"...and what is your name, little one?" asked the Navigator gently.

"I'm Chloe," she said as she crawled up one of Brave-and-Faithful's oars to come on board into the Navigator's welcoming hand. He placed her on the seat in front of him.

"I've been adrift on that leaf for quite a while. I was too close to the water's edge when the wind carried the leaf and me way out into the current. It was really pretty scary; but after hearing your voice, I feel safe again. Thanks for letting me come on board."

"That's a beautiful name," said Brave-and-Faithful.

"Yes, indeed it is," smiled the Navigator as he held Chloe close to his face.

While they conversed they began drifting closer to shore. Surprisingly Brave-and-Faithful began to revert back to Fearful-and-Doubtful. He had recognized the island as the former home of Cutter.

The Navigator took notice. "Steady," he said, putting Chloe down, then firmly gripping his oars to reassure the little boat that he was in safe hands.

"This is a very desolate looking place," said Brave-and-Faithful.

"Ah, it's not so bad," said Chloe.

"It's all in the way you look at it," said the Navigator. "Wherever you are, you are there for a purpose."

"To me, it's home," said Chloe. "Each day I explore my wonderful home a little more, but I'm so small, what could my purpose be?"

"You'll know in time."

Chloe stared at the Navigator in awe; she had never encountered anyone with so much love. It was as if her heart grew bigger and warmer inside. She began to crawl ever so cautiously toward the Navigator's face, first up his arm, then his shoulder.

"It's ok, Chloe; I will not harm you."

One leg at a time, she steadily climbed until she was inches from his face. She stared into his eyes.

"Chloe, up this close I can see so easily how cute you really are."

"Th-th-thank you." She stuttered and blushed.

"You don't have to be afraid. I'm here to tell you the Creator loves you deeply and does indeed have a purpose for you. You are not an accident. You are precious in His sight," the Navigator said.

"The Creator?"

"It is He who made you and gave you life. He made you just the way you are--- beautiful."

"But I'm a chubby caterpillar and I move so slowly. I don't even have any friends. So what's good about that?"

"You've got me," said the Navigator.

"...and me," added Brave-and-Faithful.

"Chloe, listen closely to me. I want to tell you three things, and I don't want you to ever forget them. No matter who tells you otherwise:"

You are greatly loved just as you are.

You have great value and worth, and

You were born to FLY!" He gestured with his arms opened wide.

Chloe chuckled and smiled, "Me?" She jumped as high as she could and clicked her heels together, each leg running down like a xylophone. She was extremely happy. Chloe could see in the Navigator's eyes that he was telling the truth. She started to cry tears of joy. She said quizzically: "Me? Really?"

"Yes, you were born to fly."

"Where are my wings?"

The Navigator smiled, "In time, in time."

Then she stood up on her legs and began flapping them to see if she could fly, saying: "I was born to fly! I was born to fly!" Nothing happened. "Why can't I fly now?"

The Navigator laughed, "My little friend, don't worry, you'll soon be flying, in time, in time. Till then remember my words, for they are sure and true. You were born to fly."

When Brave-and-Faithful reached the shore, the Navigator gently held his hand for Chloe to climb aboard, and then he placed his hand onto the sand. Chloe wiggled her way back to the beach

"It's time for Brave-and-Faithful and me to leave. I must keep my promise to get him to the Port of Heaven to meet the Creator," said the Navigator.

"Can I go too?"

"Not now. First you must learn to fly." He waved goodbye after he pushed off and began to row.

"Nice to meet you, Chloe!" called Brave-and-Faithful.

"Bye!" shouted Chloe, swaying as she stood up on her back two legs.

"I love you, Chloe! You can call on me, for I am always closer than you think. Remember, you were born to fly!" The Navigator's voice faded into the ever present fog that surrounded the inlet leading to the Cove of Abandonment.

From that day forth even the fog never dampened her dream of flying. Sometimes she flapped her legs in great expectation, but nothing happened. Still in her tiny tender heart, she believed and held onto the Navigator's words.

Turning back to Crow, she added: "And I remember when he touched my soft fuzzy fur; it made me arch my back and giggle. He was so much fun to be with."

Crow sat quietly, wishing he too could have the Navigator's touch.

"Well, I need to be going now, nice to have met you."

"Yeah."

"By the way, I'm Chloe. What's your name?"

"Crow."

"I like that name. It sounds strong and independent."

"You do know that I could eat you," Crow said with one raised eyebrow.

"Oh, but you won't."

"How do you know that? How can you be so sure?"

"I can see it in your eyes. Your desire for a friend is much deeper than your craving for food. You long to be loved by a true friend who genuinely cares about you."

"You can see that in my eyes?"

"Your caw is worse than your possible bite. I'll take my chances. I've got to fly now. Well, maybe not just now, but one day I will, and I'll come by and show you."

Crow looked at Chloe, still not quite knowing what to think of her. Deep in his heart he was grateful she had come by and tried to cheer him up.

As she waddled away, she began to hum her little refrain once more. At the moment she went out of sight, the sun broke through the heavy gray clouds, showering its rays directly on Crow. The sun warmed his body and his heart. Hope had started to settle deep inside. Though he couldn't put his finger on what was happening, he knew it sure felt good.

Chapter 11

Arrival at the Cove

"Are you sure that's the place?" asked Schraeder.

The closer they came to the Cove, the wind increased so much they were getting concerned about landing.

"Yes, it has to be. There's nothing else like it that we've flown over. Look how colorless it is. It's very, ah, very…"

"Desolate, and to think that Crow could be living in a place that, that, ah…"

"I know what you meeeeean!" Suddenly a thrust of wind pushed them violently downward, causing part of one wing to bend backward. They were losing altitude quickly. Their descent was leading them into the water a short distance from shore.

They cried for help. No one heard. No one answered. No one came. They began to tip to the left and steering became haphazard. They had lost control of the glider.

"Salty, lean onto my side; maybe we can right ourselves."

Suddenly, they heard a rip. They looked in fear as a seam on the right side of the wing was being slowly unraveled by the strong wind.

"What are we going to do?" cried Salty, looking at Schraeder who was also white knuckling the chest bar in front of him. They could see the white foam of the waves as they got closer.

"Push forward and lean toward the right, and you will find what you're hoping for," a voice spoke softly in their ears.

"What did you say, Salty?"

"I didn't say anything. But I heard it, too."

Without explanation, they both immediately did what they thought they had heard. They rose up and caught a more peaceful thermal that restored their control of the glider. They were only a hundred yards or so from landing. They began to count:

"Get ready, here we go. 10...9... 8...7...6...5...Whoa!" They had miscalculated. Landing rather abruptly, the glider hit a few rocks and then skimmed across the surf, coming to rest on the pebble-strewn beach. Parts of the glider were scattered around. Thankfully they still had their helmets on and had no serious injuries, other than a few bumps and bruises. The glider, however, was ruined.

As they looked over the debris, they shared their concern of how would they ever get back to Professor Watt, and what would he think of the loss of his glider?

"Whatever happens from here onward, at least we have each other," said Salty.

"Yes, I'm thankful we're both safe," answered Schraeder. "Someone must be watching over us."

They sat on a large piece of driftwood, letting their racing hearts quiet while looking back in the direction of the Beacon of Hope Lighthouse.

"I hope the Professor is ok and not too worried about us," said Salty.

After a short respite and still a little wobbly, they began to walk the beach, but no complaining was heard, only the shared concern of finding Crow.

Chapter 12

New Neighbors

Seaworthy, Alby and Shelby, having arrived earlier on the island, had already begun to scour the area for clues of Crow's whereabouts. Seaworthy was flying over the area, while Alby nosed around looking under large shrubs and bushes, calling out: "Crow, Crow. It's Alby. Where are you? Are you alright?"

Shelby decided to get back in the water and travel to the far side of the island, which was a huge contrast from the Cove. Color was everywhere. There was sunlight, clear blue skies with an occasional cloud or two, flowers of yellow, purple, blue and red. Tall tufts of wild grasses bowed at the slightest breeze, rooted deep in the sand and sprinkled between the rocky crags. And there swam two fine specimens of walrus, enjoying the waters off shore, feeding as well as playfully teasing each other. Their names: Gwendolyn and Walter.

"Will you stop that, you're driving me crazy! Stop taking my snack away from me. I swim down to get something and you swoop down right in front of me with that big old toothy grin of yours and grab it just to tease me. Then you want ME to chase YOU? No way! I'm not playing that game anymore. I've had it up to here." She raised her flipper to nose level.

"Aw, honey, come on; you know you always pick on me too." At that moment Walter let his guard down and dropped the fish.

Immediately Gwendolyn shouted: "Ha! Ha! Gotcha!;" grabbed her delectable snack before Walter knew what had happened, then swam to the shore, chuckling all the way. "I got him again," she laughed and slapped her side with a flipper.

She climbed onto a warm, rocky overhang and laid down. As she turned onto her back gazing at the skies, she sighed, "Ah, this is the life, eh, Walt? Living in the islands was always my dream and here we are all alone on our own little island. We're living the life! Eh, Walt?" A few seconds passed, "Honey?"

Walter waddled onto the beach, grabbed a rock and scratched a checkmark under Gwen's name. "That's Gwen, 34; Walter, 7. You win again, dear," he sighed.

"Oh, honey, you know I love you. We've been together a lot of years, haven't we? You should know by now, I am so much more clever than you are."

"Maybe," he paused then continued. "I just let you win because I love you so much," Walter chided his wife as he clumsily lunged his way to join his wife on the warm but rocky coastline. As he lay down next to her, she fondly put a flipper on his head then pulled on his whiskers.

"Ow!"

Then she pinged his tusks. Annoyed, he tossed his head.

"You wouldn't lie to me," she stopped with a deliberate pause, "would you?" she asked, quickly blinking her eyelashes at him. "I beat you fair and square," another pause, "Right?"

Walter turned over and sighed, "Yes, love, you beat me."

"Fair and square?"

A loud snore began to erupt from his corner of the rock. He was out like a light.

"Oh brother, why do I bother?" Gwendolyn plunged back into the sea. A huge surge of water rose into the air, hovering over Walter.

At that very moment Walter, trying to hide his laughter, could be heard quietly chuckling to himself, "I got YOU fair and square," smiling his big toothy grin.

Then suddenly, 'WHOOSH!' Gwendolyn's wave crashed down, pushing him off the rocks.

Gwendolyn bobbed up from the water. "I knew you weren't sleeping. I know all your tricks. I don't care if you answer my question or not. It's not important. We both have to admit, we enjoy each other's company."

"That we do," agreed Walter, rolling over and putting his flippers under his chin while raising his tail and staring into the eyes of his lovely bride of 60 years.

After a time of continued amusement, they returned to the shore to bask in the afternoon sun.

As they rested, totally unaware, a small creature approached them.

"I know Crow's here somewhere. This is where Cutter hung out. It's the only place he could have gone. Flight school wouldn't welcome him back after that terrible unsportsmanlike conduct against Seaworthy. He must be here. He's got to know we forgive him for having friendship with that despicable 'Cutter' and his gang. We want to help him. We want him to know he has a purpose for living, and that we really do care about him." Shelby uttered these words slowly and quietly under his breath.

Shelby wasn't watching where he was going, when a startling deep bass voice sounded out, "Can I help you?" It was Walter, pretending to have a lower voice than usual.

Shelby had accidentally crawled onto Walter's belly. He had been wondering why his vision was slowly moving up and down; now he understood.

Whack! A flipper came out of nowhere, tumbling him off the moving mound, and Shelby found himself in the sand. Walter had brushed him off, thinking it was just an irritating tick.

Shelby staggered around, groggily looking for his glasses. Realizing they were upside down on his face, he adjusted them and peered at Walter who had gone back to sleep. Shelby cautiously climbed back onto Walter and stood eyeball to eyeball with him.

"Excuse me!" He poked firmly with his claw. Walter opened his big eyes, wide open, almost the same size as Shelby. Walter and Shelby were so close that they both were startled and yelled, "WHOA!, awaking Gwen from her nap.

"What is going on here!?" rubbing her eyes with a very wide yawn as she studied Shelby. "Aw, he's so cute."

"I'm not cute. I'm a crustacean and my name is Shelby." He bowed and raised his claw in a salute of respect.

"He rudely attacked me," scowled Walter.

"I'm Gwendolyn," extending her flipper to be kissed. Shelby reached out, and with a firm handshake said: "Nice to meet you, Lady Gwendolyn," as she grinned.

"Gwen, stop with this royalty thing," groaned Walter.

"Walt, he's harmless."

"Don't let my size fool you...WALTER." Giving him his scariest wide, bug-eyed stare and with his glasses acting as a magnifying glass to enlarge his bulging eyes even more, he then added a snap of his claw to instill further fear.

Gwen and Walter began laughing and laughing. Shelby just rolled his eyes, which got them laughing even harder and longer.

"Well, excuse me. I'm on a mission. I am searching for Crow. Do you know where I may find him?"

"Crow? Who's that?" Walter asked, finally ready to listen.

"Well, let me tell you my story," Shelby began, after clearing his throat.

Gwen and Walter listened to Shelby's dramatic rendition of encounters with Cutter while with Fairhaven. Picking up a long pine needle, Walter began to pick his teeth with it, rolling it around in his mouth. Half in, half out, over and over again. Pulling it out once in a while to interject a question, but Shelby's delivery would not allow any interruptions. So he smiled, turned over and looked at Gwen, rolled his eyes, then glanced back at Shelby, who finally drew a deep breath which one would think implied a conclusion. But no, Shelby standing on his shell, continued his testimonial. Until he finished.

Silence. Just silence. Walt and Gwen looked at the little guy and shrugged at each other.

"Anything else?" Gwen asked, glancing at Shelby.

Walter glared at her in disbelief, shaking his head.

CHAPTER 13

FINDING CROW

Seaworthy flew back to Alby to report on what he had found... or not found. "No sign of Crow anywhere."

"Are you sure?"

"Nothing."

Seaworthy and Alby walked along a trodden path that wound around the mountain. While hiking, they began hashing over ideas of where Crow might be.

"Look, the trail splits off up here," said Alby. "You go that way. Holler if you find him."

"Ok." Deciding to fly to the top of the mountain cliff, Seaworthy figured he could get a better perspective of the area.

"What a view! I can see the Cove of Abandonment from here. To think this was Cutter's idea of paradise. Yuck. That guy sure had no taste. Blah!" He continued looking around.

"Whoa! Look at this. I can see the other side of the island from here. Wow! What a difference. It's beautiful down there. I've got to check that out later."

At the same time Crow was battling another day plagued with self-guilt. "I have no future, no hope because of what I've done. I can't go on anymore. Can someone help me?! Somebody! Anybody!" He screamed out in deep anguish of soul. "Does anybody hear me? Does anybody see me? Does anybody even care?" he sighed.

At that moment a scent of roses came and filled the air, interrupting his thoughts.

"I have always seen value in you," a familiar voice whispered lovingly. It was the Navigator.

Crow turned his back from the voice that harkened to him, trying to shut himself off from the forgiving voice that beckoned him to call out the name of the one who could help him. It was a name so wonderful it seemed impossible to Crow's mind that he could be loved by him.

"I can't take this anymore. I'm out of here. This is it. It's over."

Crow flew from his perch on the oak tree to go to what was known as the 'Mount of Despair.' He went there with the intent of diving off the cliff and flying full speed into the face of the mountain's jagged terrain, but a surprise awaited him. When he arrived he found...

"Seaworthy!" Quite startled, he asked: "What are you doing here?"

"I've been looking for you. I wanted to tell you I forgive you." Seaworthy stood up to stretch, he'd been sitting quite awhile scoping out the view. He continued, "We've all been worried about you. We hadn't seen you since the Navigator banished Cutter from the Sea of Life."

"Who's 'we'?" Crow asked.

"All of us. Salty, Schraeder, Shelby, Alby and yours truly," Seaworthy said with a slight gesture of his wrists.

"You shouldn't be here." Crow shook his head, sadly realizing his plans had been thwarted.

"What are you doing up here?" asked Seaworthy.

"Duh, it's my island."

"Ok. Nice view you got here." Seaworthy sat down, crossed his legs, closed his eyes and enjoyed the breeze on his feathers.

"Well, I'll see you later. How long are you staying?"

"Don't know. We just wanted to check on you and see if you wanted some company. Aren't you glad we came?" Seaworthy asked.

Shocked by all this, Crow flew off alone, not answering Seaworthy's questions. Seaworthy hadn't noticed Crow had left because he still had his eyes closed, facing into the breeze.

CHAPTER 14

CUTTER'S TORMENT

After Crow had flown back to his favorite perch, he sat wondering what was going on.

"Why did they come? To forgive me? This is too much."

Slowly he began thinking maybe Seaworthy was being honest with him and wanted to be friends. Then out of nowhere came the memories of the hidden hurts that had crushed his heart so many times before. From years ago, they came back roaring loud and clear with vivid pictures, like paintings at an art gallery with memories of rejection and disappointment. Faces and words kept bombarding his thoughts. He was again overwhelmed with agony of his soul.

The memories cried out: *"Crow! You will never be free from me. You understand me! You will always be under my control---FOREVER! Remember what you did to Brickwater, those few careless words sent him to destruction! You did it! Do you hear me? You did it!*

You killed Brickwater! It's all your fault! You are the guilty one! Did you think it would be that easy to forget me, to erase me from your memory just because you made friends with the Navigator? HA! I'm here to stay and I'm never going away."

The memory of Cutter returned and his words were burning in his ears. He wanted to call out the Navigator's name, for he remembered he had told him to call out his name and he'd come. However, the mental anguish dampened all his heart's reasonings and closed the door of opportunity once more.

A familiar scent appeared again and immediately reminded him that every time the Navigator was around, there had been a scent of roses. Then it slowly faded away. Crow turned around to see where the scent had come from, but nothing was there.

"Please don't go," he whispered.

The Navigator had been there but now had gone. Crow wept bitterly, knowing the bondage of not forgiving himself was too much for him to release on his own. He knew only the Navigator had the key to end all the torment. But the fear of further rejection held him back from a breakthrough.

Even so, the Creator had a plan, a plan of redemption and the Navigator would never give up his pursuit of Crow. He would be restored to be Karl, the real Crow. He would come alive again and breathe freely, live life abundantly and fly in freedom like he was destined to do. If only Crow could believe he could be forgiven.

CHAPTER 15

CHLOE'S NEW HOME

Upon returning to his refuge in the old oak tree, a familiar voice softly spoke, "Hey, why so glum? It's me, Chloe. Your friend."

"I don't need any friends." Crow turned away.

"You got me," said Chloe.

"I don't need you either," growled Crow.

"Boy, you're grumpy today," stated Chloe.

"I thought you were going to fly," smirked Crow.

"In time. I've got to get ready to take a nap shortly. I'm feeling kind of strange. Like something beautiful wants to come out, but I don't know how to get it out. Have you ever felt that way?" asked Chloe.

"Strange, yeah," Crow sighed, "Like right now, but it's not beautiful."

"Don't give up. I can't wait to see what you're going to become. Maybe someday we can fly together. That would be fun." Chloe glowed at the thought.

"You are always so happy and hopeful. How do you do it?" Crow turned to face Chloe, softening his countenance.

"I don't know, I guess since I met the Navigator, he's changed my life." Chloe yawned and began knitting something soft and wonderful.

Curious, Crow asked, "What are you making?"

"I'm not sure. I've never done this before." She yawned again, then curled up her legs one at a time. "Well, I'll see you when I wake up, I'm so tired all of a sudden."

She continued weaving her little cocoon and gradually sealed herself in, but just before she closed herself off from the world, she softly whispered: "Nighty, night." She was gone. Her little home was all enclosed. Crow just stared and walked around it, admiring how well-crafted it was.

"Nighty, night... my friend." Crow whispered fondly while gently stroking her fragile pod-like dwelling.

CHAPTER 16

BACK TOGETHER

"Are you going to sleep the day away?" Shelby asked. "Gwen, since when did we get an alarm clock?" asked Walter.

"Shelby, give us a little more time. We'll see you later." Gwen politely said.

"ZZZ," added Walter.

Shelby, a little bit ruffled but nonetheless bid them 'adieu,' and crawled toward the Cove to reunite with his friends, wondering if anyone had located Crow.

"Shh," signed Seaworthy to Alby with his wing. They both laid low in the tall grass. Shelby wandered by mumbling when, "HEY! SHELBY! WHAT 'CHA DOING?"

Shelby leaped into the air, did a triple flip and landed face down into the sand. Shelby massaged his neck and then crawled back into his shell.

"Gotcha, Shelby, old buddy." Seaworthy picked up Shelby and brushed him off. "Did you hurt yourself?

"Shelby, we're sorry, we were just playing with you. That's what friends do sometimes. But if you don't like it, then we won't do it anymore, because that's what friends also do, Alby explained.

Shelby sighed, "Ok." He crawled out, bumping his head on his shell, "Umph!," rubbed his head with his claw, and asked: "Any word of Crow?"

"Seaworthy saw him yesterday, but he took off. So we're back where we started. I think he may have returned to the Cove. He knows we're all here and that we want to see him."

"Well, let's go before he takes off again," said Shelby.

"Are you saying that you want us to pick you up and carry you to the Cove with us?"

"Yes, I am. Alby, get the basket. I trust you more than somebody else I know."

"Ok, climb aboard." Alby scooped him up.

Shelby got ready for another ride. Off they went, flying over the Mount of Despair, descending toward the beach at the Cove.

Upon landing, Shelby was delighted to get out of the basket and feel the warm sand on his shell. "Smooth flight for a change. Thanks, Alby."

"A pleasure," said Alby.

"What do you guys want?" It was Crow perched on a branch high above them. He reluctantly flew down to meet them.

"We came to say we forgive you for the things you did with Cutter. And we want to be your friends," said Alby sincerely.

"Us too!" shouted Salty and Schraeder, running down the beach. "We've been looking for you too."

Seaworthy, Alby and Shelby were excited to see Salty and Schraeder.

"How did you get here?"

"It's a long story," said Schraeder.

"But a good one," added Salty.

"Well, it was a waste of your time," said Crow as he flew away.

Seaworthy was about to fly after him when Alby lightly grabbed his wing and said, "Let him have some time alone to think about all that's been said to him today. For now we should probably find a place to sleep."

"I'm getting cold," said Salty.

"Let's get a fire going," said Schraeder.

"I saw some driftwood over there," said Alby.

"Seaworthy, you and Salty go find some more dry wood, twigs and branches," said Schraeder.

"Who's going to start the fire?" asked Shelby.

"I will," said Schraeder.

"Wow! There's a lot I don't know about you," said Salty.

Schraeder smiled. After the wood was brought in, in no time at all he had a roaring fire going on the beach.

"This is amazing. It feels so good. Thanks, Schraeder." Each one agreed in his own grateful way.

"So, how did you get here anyway?" questioned Crow, returning to his visitors.

"It's a long story," started Schraeder, "but the short version is that we used Professor Watt's glider; and as you can see," pointing toward the wreckage, "we sorta crash landed."

Chapter 17

Songs of Remembrance

In the light of the full moon, wistful little melodies were carried with the wind, as if played by an orchestra from barren tree limbs. The trees may have been old and dying, and the bark may have been cracked and dry, but the music drifted upward toward the stars. A symphony rose above the dark and shadowy midnight shore of the Cove of Abandonment. The sound, carried further by the waves of the crashing sea, gently soothed all the somber sand and humanity.

Alby recognized the song. He began to hum along. Tears formed in his eyes. "This was my mother's song that she sang as she hovered over me in my shell as I broke forth into the world."

"What a precious memory," said Salty, sadly wishing she had one to recall. The wind swirled around and around, again and again, and now it brought a different melody. Salty began laughing and giggling for now she too recognized a song from long ago.

"This reminds me of playing with my brothers and sisters when we were very young." She fell down laughing and laughing, louder and louder as each refrain rose in the lilt of the wind, as if tickling her.

Then surprisingly Crow emerged from the darkness and came near the fire. No one said anything; everyone was watching Salty. The wind died down to a quiet hush, then for a moment Crow's sullenness disappeared. However as quick as he recognized that the music had gone, it came back. The music was slow and as quiet as a butterfly's wings.

Then silence. The wind was gone.

The waves slowed their tempo and gently caressed the shore. A strange looking shell was tumbling its way out of the sea, being pushed ever so carefully onto the beach, rolling forward, then pulled a little back, each wave bringing it closer and closer. Then, "whoosh", a larger wave pushed the shell out of reach of the ocean's grasp. The shell paused, motionless, and nestled softly into the sand.

Crow walked over, smelled it, kicked it over, and then he thought he heard something.

"What was that?" he said quietly, turning to the others huddling around the fire.

"Looks like an old abandoned home to me," said Shelby as he gave it a quick inspection, then added, "Not one of mine," as he crawled away.

"Did you hear anything?" asked Crow anxiously.

"All I heard was the ocean behind me."

"Looks like a conch shell," Alby stated, confidently walking toward it.

Crow bent over and strained to listen, did it indeed say something? Could a shell talk? He heard it again this time as if in a whisper. It grew clearer as he drew it closer to his ear.

"You are loved." It spoke tenderly in a way only a mother could.

"You are loved." There it was again. And yet again: "You are loved."

Crow began to cry. He picked up the shell and sat down on the beach with his legs stretched out in front of him, using one wing to support himself.

"You are loved," it continued to repeat.

"What's the matter?" asked Seaworthy.

They all bent down to hear what the shell was saying, then each one stood up in amazement.

"It's --- my mother's voice." Again it echoed, "You are loved."

At that moment Crow's heart began melting away years of hardness. "How can you say that?" Crow, wanting to believe, shouted at the shell as he put it down.

Seaworthy started walking toward Crow when Salty said, "Your mother loves you, Crow, and so do we. You just never let us in."

"You've kept us at a distance." said Schraeder.

"You can be a part of our family, if you want to," said Seaworthy.

Schraeder walked over, gave Crow an unexpected hug, followed by Salty.

Crow couldn't help being overwhelmed by the continuing voice of his mother coming from the shell, "You are loved." He continued crying, dropping the shell, and surprisingly welcomed the hugs.

No words could express what was happening inside Crow's heart and mind. He broke from the hug and tenderly picked up the shell, once more hearing,

"You are loved."

The wind began to build and the trees began to sing a new song. It was a melody that only Crow remembered, a song his mom and dad sang to him when he was a young bird. He began to sing along with the precious memory with his voice occasionally fading and cracking.

"You are loved, you are loved

Forever in our hearts, you are loved.

No one will ever take your place,

Where you are in our hearts.

For you are loved, you are loved.

Forever in our hearts, you are loved."

The wind died down and the orchestra drifted away, leaving only the sound of the waves and the faint refrain from the shell harmonizing with Crow, "You are loved."

Crow flew away, leaving his hoped-for friends behind, returning to his favorite perch. It was night and he chose to go to sleep. Yet every once in awhile he peeked to see if the shell was still on the beach, shining in the moonlight.

Shelby crawled by and gave the shell a tap once more.

No response.

He paused, "hmm," then went on his way.

CHAPTER 18

AN EMERGING BUTTERFLY

In the late morning hours Crow heard a strange crackling like dry leaves being stepped upon. The strange noise was coming from where Chloe had last sealed herself into a cocoon. But now it was shimmying and shaking. Something was breaking forth from the inside out. Suddenly a beautiful, brilliant rainbow of colors emerged. It was Chloe! She had big colorful wings, and she smiled at Crow as she yawned and fluttered down, softly landing next to him.

"Hi, Crow." She yawned again. "How are you? What a great sleep I had. I didn't know I was so tired. I feel really refreshed."

"Chloe, you're a butterfly. You look... you look beautiful and you have wings now. Where did they come from?"

Just then Chloe noticed her wings. "Oooh, are they nice!" she gasped in surprise. She began stretching them up and down, and then it happened...she began to fly!

"Crow, I'm flying! I'm flying! Like the Navigator said!!! I told you I was born to fly!! Whee!"

Crow was speechless. He watched in utter amazement as Chloe jumped off the branch and headed into the breeze. It carried her up higher and higher.

"Whee!" she yelled with excitement. "I can fly!!! The Navigator was right."

"Thank you, Navigator," she said, not knowing if she would be heard.

Seaworthy flew up to visit with Crow after noticing all the commotion going on.

Chloe flew down and hovered, saying, "Hi, I'm Chloe and I can fly."

"Hi, I'm Seaworthy and I can fly too. Let's fly together."

"Come on, Crow, fly with us."

They began flying with Chloe celebrating her debut flight. What a marvelous sight to behold.

They returned to the tree and sat and talked some more. All of a sudden Chloe sneezed. She sneezed something very unusual - she sneezed a rainbow of colors which changed the atmosphere wherever she would go. She noticed after she sneezed that it made Crow smile, something he hadn't done in a long time, and it made Seaworthy chuckle.

Crow thought, "Friends" and then breathed a sigh of gratitude. The fragrance of roses piqued his attention. He heard within his heart, "Your real name is Karl. That's who you really are." The thought revealed the true person he really was.

"Karl," the voice called again, "You are loved."

"Karl, Karl." A smile came to his beak and he said, "I like my name. Karl."

The Navigator appeared before Karl.

"This is family?" Karl questioned, pointing to all his friends around him, Salty, Schraeder, Alby, Seaworthy and Chloe. They were all very appreciative, for the Navigator had used each of them in his plan to set Karl free from his heavy burden. Each had a hard time containing the tears caused by their overwhelming joy.

A surprised visitor watched from high above, perched on a nearby banyan tree. He smiled and wiped his glasses, putting them back on, though beginning to fog up again from his tearful flow.

"Karl... I like that name," said Professor Watt as he flew down to join the group.

"Me too," smiled Karl with a sigh of relief, "me too." He had begun to find the forgiveness he longed for.

CHAPTER 19

LOVELY

L ater in the morning, quiet sobbing could be heard coming from behind the giant boulders jutting out into the bay. A swan swam by, her head hanging low, occasionally flipping tears off her beak into the water.

"Hello. What's wrong?"

She was startled to see that someone saw her when she was her most vulnerable.

"I'm..." he paused, taken aback by her beauty. "...Karl. What's your name?"

The rest of the group, gathered behind the rocks, was delighted to hear him refer to himself as Karl. A beautiful change was occurring.

As she glided effortlessly toward shore, regaining her composure, she murmured, "My name is 'Lovely.'"

"Why are you so down, and why are you alone? You're so, so..." he gulped. "Beautiful. You should have lots of friends."

She began to cry once more. "Everyone used to like being around me because they thought I'm pretty, but ... she started to swim away.

"Please don't go," Karl urged. "But what?"

Lovely stopped and turned around. "I'm not perfect."

"What do you mean?"

She swam closer, feeling a genuine sense of caring from Karl. She approached the shore, gathering up the courage to face the usual expected stares and ridicule. "But this", she replied, hobbling out of the water. She stood there, one leg weaker and shorter than the other, awaiting his gawking and ridicule.

"Well, aren't you going to laugh and stare at me?" she spouted angrily, tears flowing down. "I knew it, you're just like my friends. I can swim just fine, and I can fly, but I walk funny."

"My friends, if that's what they really were, abandoned me like a plague. I didn't ask to be born this way."

Karl's friends began to emerge to meet Lovely.

"Oh, my!" She was startled.

"We're Karl's friends," said Seaworthy.

Alby could tell her leg had become a point of insecurity concerning her true identity and value.

Salty, with paws on her hips, looked at Schraeder and said, "What's she got that I ain't got?"

"Wings." Seaworthy said innocently.

They all laughed, even Lovely had to laugh between her tears.

"Thanks, guys. I needed that." She exhaled a sigh of relief.

"'Guys'? I'm a lady, too," said Salty with a tomboyish air. "Maybe you didn't notice." She fluffed up her tail, tickling Schraeder's nose, who immediately sneezed.

"I'm sorry," Lovely replied. "Yes, you are and you're adorably cute, too."

"AH, well, um..." Salty stuttered, blushing, flattered by Lovely's kind and unexpected response. "Thanks."

"Now darlin', you're gonna be just fine." It was Gwendolyn coming out of the water. She and Walter had been swimming by and overheard Lovely's story.

"Hi, everyone! I'm Gwendolyn, call me Gwen; and this is Walter." She pointed with her flipper, but Walt was not nearby, he was still swimming. "Walter, get over here. Meet these nice folks. You must be friends of Shelby's. We met him awhile ago when he was searching for someone named..."

"Crow," said Walter, joining Gwen on shore. "Hi, I'm Walt."

Everyone began introducing themselves. Then Karl said, "I was Crow, but my real name is Karl; and this is our new friend, Lovely."

"It's nice to meet you all."

"She looks beautiful just the way she is, don't you think so, Walter? Walter? Oh, that Walter. Walter!? Where are you?"

Walter had gone swimming again but not alone. He had taken Schraeder, Seaworthy and Shelby for a cruise. They were comfortably resting on his belly, enjoying their expedition while Walter was floating on his back, drifting in the current.

"This is kind of like traveling with Fairhaven," said Seaworthy.

"Fairhaven?" asked Walter.

Shelby began reminding him of their old friend, saying "Seaworthy, this is not quite the same as sailing with Fairhaven..."

"But it's a close second!" interrupted Schraeder.

That got Walter laughing, which made Shelby 'plop' into the water. "Oops! Sorry, little guy."

"Walter, get back here. Can't you see this little lady needs some attention," scolded Gwen.

"Lovely, you are beautiful," said Karl shyly, stricken nearly speechless by her beauty.

"Me? No. Without this," looking down at her leg, "I might be beautiful."

"Look how your feathers glisten with the dew in the early morning sunlight. It's amazing, shall I say it again? Beautiful. It speaks of your uniqueness," Karl stated.

"But I don't feel beautiful," she said, frustrated.

"Beauty is best seen by others, not necessarily as seen by ourselves," said Alby.

"And your acts of kindness aren't for public display because they come from your heart. It's like when you helped that little bird build her nest. She had hurt her shoulder and you had compassion on her. That is the type of beauty that never fades away, it only increases."

Everyone was amazed at the words of encouragement that flowed from Karl.

"How did you know that?" Lovely asked, shocked.

Karl gulped. "I was flying around the island one day and saw you. I hid among the leaves of a tree and watched you. You were very kind to that little one. I was envious. I have always wanted to be that kind of friend."

Shelby came on shore, water flowing from his shell. "Walter, thanks for the ride!" he sputtered.

"Walt," Gwen nudged him and directed his eyes to Shelby.

"Oh, I'm sorry about that. I didn't mean to dump you."

Shelby found a comfortable spot, and curled up inside his shell, only his eyes peeking out. His eyes closed as he fell asleep with his glasses cockeyed; then snoring began to echo from his home.

"Aw, he looks so cute, doesn't he, Walter?" said Gwen.

"Yes, dear," said Walter half-heartedly agreeing with her, while letting Schraeder and Seaworthy disembark as he reached the shore.

"I've got to be going," said Lovely as she entered the water and paddled out. "Thanks for your friendship!" as she headed down the coastline.

"Bye, come and see us again!" They all waved goodbye.

"You can be a part of our family anytime if you want to, you can never have too much family," Seaworthy called out.

Lovely waved in reply.

"Gwen, let's get going, it's almost lunchtime," Walter said.

"Is that all you think about? Food?" asked Gwen, a little perturbed.

"And you." He smiled.

"Aw, honey babe." She smiled back at him.

The gang at the beach all roared with laughter and teased Walter, "Honey babe! Whoa! Whoa! Whoa!!"

Looking at everyone she sighed, "He's so sweet..." then she looked at her hubby and added "at times." She smiled back at them. "See you all later," as she headed off to catch up with Walter.

"Bye."

Then everyone in unison called out, "Bye, honey babe!" Followed by lots of giggles and laughter.

Chapter 20

A Surprise Visitor

"What are we going to do now?" asked Seaworthy.

"I'm going..." Alby was interrupted.

"Hi, everyone." It was the Navigator.

"Where'd you come from?" asked Salty quizzically. Everyone was happily surprised to see him.

Seaworthy ran up and gave him a big hug and asked, "How's Fairhaven?"

"He's doing fine."

"Tell him we all say 'hello,'" said Shelby shaking off the sand and making his way toward him.

"What brings you here today? You just missed our new friends Lovely, Gwendolyn and Walter," said Seaworthy.

"I'm sure they'll be back and you can meet them the next time," said Schraeder.

"I came to see Crow," said the Navigator.

"It's Karl now," said Seaworthy.

"Why, yes, it is," he replied.

Karl turned around and started slowly walking away, not wanting to look into the Navigator's eyes.

"Karl," the Navigator called out, running to catch up to him. "Come with me. I want to show you something."

Seaworthy started to walk after them, but Alby stopped him, saying to all of them, "I think we need to give them some time alone. Let's head over to see how Lovely is doing."

They all agreed, except for Shelby who was interested in a butterfly that had landed on his shell. It was Chloe, enjoying the comraderie she was observing among all the friends.

Seaworthy, Salty, Schraeder and Alby headed out. "We'll see you later, Shelby."

Chapter 21

The Search Party

The Navigator and Karl walked together, with Karl occasionally glancing up at him apprehensively. The Navigator calmly reached out his arm, suggesting that Karl hop up to be carried. Reluctantly he did. The Navigator began to stroke his back. Karl welcomed it and relaxed more and more in his presence.

The sun was reflecting off the ocean with clear blue skies, the tranquil day began blurring the line between where the plush forest ended and the turquoise water began. The surrounding beauty was mirrored in the passive waters of the secluded inlet, far from the austere bleakness of the Cove of Abandonment.

As they walked, the Navigator spoke: "You don't remember me, but we used to play together when you were young, it was even before flight school. You've always been my friend."

Tears slowly streaked down Karl's face. He had forgotten. Gradually that memory returned. As he remembered, the eyes of his heart began to be unveiled. He beheld the Navigator in his fullness of love and kindness. He felt accepted. Joy flooded his heart.

The Navigator stopped and pointed to a small isolated pool of water. He said, "Karl, look into the water. What do you see?"

The water became like a movie screen. "It's my mom and dad. They look worried and sad. Are they ok?"

"Yes."

"What are they doing?"

"They're desperately searching for you."

"But, I thought they abandoned me. I haven't seen them for 6 years. Six years! Navigator, that's a long time." He cried, covering his face in anguish.

"They've never stopped looking for you. They've never stopped loving you. They were held back because a storm injured your mother on their way back to see you at flight school."

"Mom! Dad!" Karl cried out, falling to his knees. Deep groans of longings suppressed over the years began to gush from the depths of his heart.

The picture faded. Karl turned to look at the Navigator. "I miss them so much."

"They miss you, too." The Navigator opened his arms to embrace Karl, turning his fears into hope.

Chapter 22

Chloe Meets a New Friend

Shelby, sensing something on top of his shell, peered out and noticed a butterfly had settled to rest for a while.

"And who are you?" Shelby asked, a little indignant while adjusting his glasses and rising out of his sand bunker.

"Oh, OH!" exclaimed Chloe, startled by the movement. "I'm sorry. I thought that this was just a vacant shell."

"Well, it's not!" he replied sharply. He began to eye Chloe hovering in front of him, flapping her beautifully colored wings.

"Ah-choo!" She giggled after she had sneezed a glowing rainbow of colors.

When Shelby saw the colors, his countenance changed. "Wow! That was really...wow." He was at a loss for words. "I'm Shelby."

"Hi, I'm Chloe. You have a very nice home."

"Thank you. Do you live here?"

"Yes."

"Do you know Karl? He lives here, too," Shelby asked.

"In there?" Chloe said, pointing to his shell.

"No, no, but here on the island," responded Shelby, shaking his head side to side.

"Oh." Chloe said, smiling at her silly question. "No, I don't know him. Do you know Crow?"

"Yes, that's him. His real name is Karl."

"Karl?"

"It's a long story, but a good one."

"Is he ok?"

"Oh, yes, he is doing much better."

"How do you know him?"

"It's also a long story, but a good one too."

They both chuckled.

"Look! Here he comes with the Navigator. They went for a walk earlier."

"The Navigator? He's the one who told me when I was just a little caterpillar that I would fly one day, and look at me now!" She fluttered away, rejoicing to see Karl and the Navigator. Shelby followed along.

"Hi, Karl! Hi, Navigator! Look at me. Whee! Thank you, Navigator, for believing in me."

"It's all because you believed in me," said the Navigator fondly. "Did you notice my surprise gift to you?"

"Gift?" questioned Chloe.

"What happens when you sneeze?"

"Colors! They illuminate around me."

"That's it. Those colors affect others in your presence with hope, love, joy, peace and kindness.

"So that's what happened," Shelby said, approaching the Navigator. "I was agitated at Chloe at first and then my attitude left, it just kind of went away after she sneezed. Then I felt a kindness come all over me."

"Yes, that was my gift to you, Chloe."

"Why me?"

"I thought you'd like it."

"I do." She sneezed again. The colors rose up into the breeze and dissipated, leaving the four of them smiling.

"Karl, I thought your name was Crow?" Chloe inquired.

"It was, but that's not who I really am. Something's changing inside me. I'm not who I used to be."

"Well, that's good to hear," said Seaworthy, returning. "Hi, I'm Seaworthy. You're lovely."

"No, I'm Chloe. Lovely is a swan. She's one of my friends. Like you...Karl."

Turning to the Navigator she said, "Karl knew me when I was just a caterpillar. We had a nice visit a while back."

"You have changed, Chloe. I'm glad to see you flying and your colors are out of this world. You look great!"

A quick flash of rainbow colors fanned across her wings from left to right, revealing bashfulness. A tender gust of wind blew her upward, carrying her in a gentle movement like a conductor's baton directing an orchestra.

Seaworthy looked up at her, "That looks like fun."

"Oh, it is, it is," she responded. Chloe got lost in the moment. Seaworthy flew up to be with her, and they began laughing together.

"Karl," said the Navigator, looking at him as he enjoyed Chloe's beautiful agility in the breeze. "That's what I'm beginning to do in you. Something so wonderful that it will take your breath away in an astounding moment. I've got to be going for now, but I'll see you again."

Karl looked back at the Navigator, but he was already gone.

Chloe floated down, "I'm so glad to see you are doing better. You had me worried."

"Yeah, I feel much better. Hopeful anyway. But I don't know what is going on inside of me. I'm excited, then I'm doubtful, then I get confused when I try to figure it out."

"Don't try to figure it out. Don't worry, the Navigator only gives good gifts."

CHAPTER 23

A FAMILY OF FRIENDS

Salty and Schraeder ran down the beach to meet up with Karl. "Where's the Navigator? We saw you with him."

"He just left."

"He'll be back again," encouraged Alby, as he saw their disappointed faces as he joined them.

"Where's Professor Watt?" Schraeder inquired.

"He's getting ready to return to the Beacon of Hope Lighthouse. He was so glad to see you were both safe," said Alby. "He said he'll see you before he leaves."

"How was your time with the Navigator, Karl?"

"It was wonderful. Better than I can explain. It was an experience I'll never forget. Such love and acceptance. I think he really does care about me. He showed me pictures in a puddle of water reflecting my mom and dad. They ARE looking for me!"

"Pretty cool," said Seaworthy. "He's fun like that."

"Almost like the voice in the shell," said Alby.

"Yeah, but that was just a shell that washed up..." He stopped midsentence. "Do you think the Navigator did that too?"

Alby smiled.

"Wow," Karl said as he realized that the Navigator would do such a wonderful thing.

Suddenly Karl ran down the beach, frantically turning over shell after shell, longing to hear the sweet refrain of his mother's words, "You are loved."

After a while, "Did you find it?" Shelby asked.

"No, but I will always remember its message: "You are loved."

Each day the group of friends saw gradual changes in Karl that overjoyed them all. He had begun to see he was not the cause of Brickwater's death, thus releasing him from false guilt. He also started to understand and to receive the forgiveness the group genuinely offered. He had accepted their invitation to be part of the growing family of friends. Most importantly, he was learning to forgive himself.

CHAPTER 24

SEARCHING FOR LOVELY

A few days had gone by when Salty questioned: "Has anybody seen Lovely?"

No one had. "I want to go look for her, I'm worried about her. Anybody want to join me?"

"OK, I'll go," said Schraeder.

"I'll go too," volunteered Seaworthy.

The three set off down the beach. Not long after they began their journey they found a beaten path through the tall grass and dead branches.

"Let's go up this way," Schraeder eagerly suggested.

"It doesn't look too safe." A surprisingly different response came from Salty.

"Come on, it looks like a mysterious hidden pathway to a world far beyond our comprehension. Ha, Ha, Ha." Seaworthy humorously chanted with a sinister laugh.

Schraeder and Seaworthy cleared the path and saw that it led uphill toward the top of the mountain. As they traveled, they spoke about Lovely when...

Salty said, "I think that's her right there." Pointing a long way off, Seaworthy pulled out the binoculars he borrowed from Schraeder. Studying the shoreline, he saw that it was Lovely. They yelled and shouted, but she couldn't hear them.

They began to run, excited to catch up to her. Seaworthy led the way, the binoculars bouncing from side to side, causing him to stumble. The other two were following so closely that they too fell down, tumbling over and over again down the grassy field. Sizing up their bumps and bruises, they decided to give up the search mission and tended to each other. They were ok and were able to laugh at their experience.

"Whew! That was a trip! No pun intended," said Seaworthy.

"You got that right," agreed Schraeder.

Seaworthy pulled out the now badly dented binoculars and checked the shoreline again, but no sign of Lovely.

CHAPTER 25

CAMPFIRE

Meanwhile, back at the beach, Lovely swam by and stopped for a visit. "Hi! How is everyone?"

Karl spoke first, "Doing fine. How about you?"

"I'm doing much better since I met you all. Thank you for your kindness the other day," Lovely replied.

"How do you feel about yourself now?" Karl asked.

"Well, it's part of me, but it doesn't dictate who I really am. It did once but no longer. Many thanks to you."

Chloe spoke up, "Did you see Salty, Schraeder and Seaworthy? They were looking for you this afternoon."

"No, I didn't."

"No need to worry," said Alby. "That Schraeder is pretty clever and has a good sense about him. They'll be fine."

Professor Watt came by and surprised everyone. Alby introduced Chloe and Lovely to the Professor. They all sat on the beach and shared stories of their travels on the Sea of Life. The sun began setting, but still no sign of the others.

Chloe said, "What shall we do for them? Should we go and look for them before the night fully falls?"

"We could scout for them by flying over the island," Karl suggested.

"Good idea," said Alby, echoed by the Professor.

"I can go, too. I can fly." Lovely spread her wings.

"Oooh!" Everyone was astounded by her magnificent wing span.

They each took different directions, Shelby staying behind to watch for the return of the missing trio. When asked if he wanted to go or stay, Shelby declared, "I don't like to fly, thank you very much! I'll be happy to stay."

When the skies began to darken, Alby, Lovely and Karl had each noticed a little fire on the hilltop. Surprisingly they found Seaworthy, Schraeder and Salty happy as could be, laughing and singing around a small campfire.

Lovely landed first. "Hi, guys. We've been worried about you."

"And we've been worried about you," they smiled. "We tripped and fell, and then decided to rest our bumps and bruises. Now that it's almost night, we figured we might as well get comfortable and head back in the morning."

Professor Watt and Alby landed next. "Hey, you three! Glad to see you're all ok."

"Hi, Professor, how are you? We've been missing you." Salty and Schraeder ran to greet him with a warm friendly hug.

"Well, I'm doing much better since finding you," he responded. "But I can only stay for a short visit. I've got to get back to the Beacon of Hope Lighthouse."

"Professor Watt," Schraeder paused, swallowed, and worked up the courage to say...

"Go on, tell him." Salty poked him. "Go on."

"Tell me what?" the Professor asked, very curious.

"Salty and I want to talk with you about something," continued Schraeder.

"Well, what is it? You have my full attention."

"Ok, let's go over here," said Salty, locking her paws with the Professor and Schraeder.

"Professor," said Schraeder, beginning to perspire. "We... ah... we've been thinking. Ah... we want to... a..."

"We want to be Lighthouse Keepers," stated Salty, not able to hold it in any longer.

"Like you," added Schraeder, their eyes wide open, hopefully waiting for a positive response.

"Well, what a surprise," said the Professor, very moved.

"A good surprise?" asked Salty.

"Oh, yes, a very good surprise." The Professor paused, gained his composure, and then continued, "There is a lot of training that you will have to learn."

"Will you teach us? We're ready," they said in unison, standing to attention and saluting their fatherly friend with respect. "Please."

"I would be honored to. You can stand at ease."

"When can we start?" Salty asked.

"You can start when we all get back to the Beacon of Hope. I'll head out now and make some preparations ready for your return." Professor Watt flew off as Salty and Schraeder rushed back to the campfire to tell their friends their news. Everyone was delighted at their decision.

"A very honorable vocation,"said Alby approvingly.

Salty suddenly jumped up in despair. "How are we going to get back to the Beacon of Hope? Our glider is broken."

"We'll help you think of a way. Don't fret about it now. Take one day at a time," encouraged Alby.

Then in came Karl. "Schraeder, you sure do know how to make a good campfire. It feels great," he said as he warmed up his wings and backside.

Alby spoke up, "Let's all spend the night here."

"Sure, there's lots of room," said Seaworthy, glancing around in the light of the fire. "We're all family, right?"

"That's right," said Karl with a smile, "We're family."

"Where's Chloe?" remarked Karl, concerned.

"Haven't seen her since we left the beach," said Alby.

"I hope she's ok," said Lovely.

CHAPTER 26

THE FAMILY UNITES

Chloe had been having a difficult time flying because the evening breeze had picked up. She couldn't make much headway.

Lovely said, "I'm going after Chloe."

"I'm coming with you," said Salty.

"But, you can't fly."

"With you I can."

"Alright then, hop aboard and let's go."

Within seconds they were entering the darkening skies around the island, searching for Chloe.

"Let's fly by Gwen and Walter; maybe they've seen her."

"Good idea."

Shortly afterward they spotted the walruses, and circling above them, Salty called out, "Have you seen Chloe?"

Both agreed that they had not but would keep their eyes out for her and she would be safe with them if they found her.

"Check in with us in the morning; we'd like to know if you found her or if you need our help," said Gwen, as Salty and Lovely continued on their flight.

"Let's check the Cove of Abandonment," suggested Salty.

"Ok, hold on, making a right turn."

"Whoa! This is fun. Can we do this again some other time?"

"Sure."

"We're like sisters, you know."

Lovely smiled. "There it is. I'll drop down lower."

They both began to yell out Chloe's name. "Chloe! Chloe!" No answer.

They returned to the beach to check in with Shelby, who was in charge of the home base. Upon arrival they discovered Chloe and Shelby in a delightful conversation.

"Now have you heard the one about the two crustaceans that..."

"Well, there you are," said a relieved Salty and Lovely as Salty slid from Lovely's back.

"Hi, the winds picked up and I couldn't go very far, so I returned to hang out with Shelby till everyone returned."

"So glad you're safe," said Lovely.

"I see you found Salty. Where's everybody else?" asked Shelby.

"Schraeder started a campfire and Alby thought it would be fun to stay overnight on the mountain together."

"Chloe, do you want to come?" asked Salty.

"Yes, I do. I'm a little chilly here. How about you, Shelby?" asked Chloe.

"I can give you a ride," said Lovely. "Come with us. Salty, hold on to our precious cargo," she said, looking at Chloe.

Chloe giggled and laughed and then sneezed. The colors couldn't be seen but it did change Shelby's response to one of, "I'll go, too, but let it be known...I don't like flying."

"Well, it's the only option you've got," said Salty.

"Ok, ok, Lovely, I'll go. What do you want me to do?"

"Open your front door. Go to the back of your home. I will put one of my feet inside and carry you that way. Are you ready?"

"Huh?" Shelby wasn't ready for what happened next. A giant foot invaded his property, bursting through his front door and thrusting him against a wall.

"This certainly is not lovely," he grunted as he gasped for fresh air. "Oof, ah, ow, umph, yuck..."

"Oh yes, it's me," Lovely responded, preparing to fly. Off they went. As they took off, Shelby said in a muffled voice, "That's not what I meant."

Shortly they landed at the campfire with their friends. Everyone was glad to be together again, knowing that no one was harmed, even Shelby.

"Ah Choo!" Chloe sneezed as she flew out of the safety of Salty's tender paw, bringing forth joy and laughter which by now had become the usual expectation, one they still greatly enjoyed. Schraeder pulled out his red bandana and wrapped Chloe in it to help her get warm.

Everyone settled around the fire, occasionally poking it and sending sparks flying into the night sky.

CHAPTER 27

THE FORMER COVE REVISITED

A voice emerged out of the darkness. "Hello, everyone!" It was the Navigator!

"Hi, Navigator," everyone responded to his unexpected arrival, wondering what he was going to talk about tonight.

"We love it when you're with us," Seaworthy said. They all agreed wholeheartedly.

"This is Lovely. I don't think you've met her yet," said Karl, putting his wing around her back and presenting her to meet him.

"I am pleased to meet you," said the Navigator very graciously.

"Thank you," she responded shyly.

"What brings you here tonight?" asked Alby.

"I came by tonight to share some history about this place."

"What about this place?" asked Karl.

"Ah Choo!" sneezed Chloe, once more causing even the Navigator to laugh and respond. "Bless you! Such a loud sneeze from one as dainty as you," he added with a smile.

When she sneezed, as it blew into the fire, it sent sparks of rainbow colors into the night sky. They quieted down and turned their attention to the Navigator as he began...

"The Cove of Abandonment wasn't always like this. It used to be filled with vibrant flowers, and trails like jigsaw pieces running throughout the island. It was a place of great joy, excitement and adventure. But everything changed when Cutter arrived."

Karl dropped his head, not wanting to make eye contact with the Navigator.

"Alby remembers."

"Yes, I do. Navigator, remember the slide on the ridge overlooking the cove? We'd climb up and then slide all the way down into the refreshing water. What a ride!" Turning to Seaworthy, he added: "You'd love it!"

Alby talked about it with such enthusiasm that you would have thought he was 30 years younger.

"This used to be," continued the Navigator, "the recreation area of your flight school, Karl and Seaworthy."

"No way!" exclaimed Seaworthy, jumping to his feet. "Karl, we've got to find that slide!"

Karl was still a little reserved.

"No need to rush." said Alby, bursting at the seams. "I found it the other day while we were looking for Crow. I mean, Karl."

The Navigator continued on, "When Cutter came, the mood of the island shifted from joy and laughter to domination and control. He forced everyone off half the island to set up his personal lair. Gradually the colors faded to a dismal gray. The desolation is still creeping, and eventually will overtake the entire island."

"Can it be stopped?" asked Salty.

"Can you bring it back to the way it was?" questioned Schraeder.

"A place of adventure?" begged Seaworthy.

"A place of peace and quiet?" whispered Shelby.

Silence. Everyone looked at Shelby, who shrugged, nervously smiled, adjusted his glasses, then stated: "Good night," and crawled back into his shell.

"Yes, I can do all of that," said the Navigator. "But it will take a change of heart."

"A change of heart?" Karl asked, raising his head from his wings that were resting on his knees.

"Yes, but all of you must work together as a team and not let any offense or unforgiveness fester in your hearts toward one another. Each of you is accountable for your own heart's actions. In the morning I want each of you to go separately to a place where you can be alone and think to yourself, 'Have I offended anyone? Is there anyone I need to forgive?'"

Then, turning to Karl, "and... have I forgiven myself?" He handed Karl a dried, decayed leaf. As he picked it up and extended it to Karl, it came back to life, becoming a beautiful waxy green, flexible leaf. "Just like this. This can happen to you."

Turning back to the others, "Remember, the Creator loves each one of you and desires to see you enjoy each other's company and to respect one another."

The Navigator disappeared as he said the last few words while everyone looked at Karl's green leaf. But as soon as the Navigator left, it became crumbly. One by one the fragments were carried away by a puff of wind.

Each one suddenly had an awareness of what the Navigator meant. Love changes everything. The Navigator demonstrated the Creator's love by making the leaf green and then having it wither away when he was gone.

"I think what he's saying to us is this," said Alby. "If we keep close to the Navigator, the Creator's love will pour out to us and through us, and our lives will not dry up but be filled with life."

Silence filled the campsite. Each one settled down for the night and gradually began to doze, dreaming of what the Navigator had spoken.

CHAPTER 28

A DREAM IN THE NIGHT

In the middle of the night, Karl began tossing and turning, randomly uttering a word or two. In a dream, he saw an image appear, first rather blurry then gradually coming into focus and it spoke to him: "Who loves you, honey?"

As the image continued to become clearer, the voice repeated, "Who loves you, honey?"

Then the picture was crystal clear. It was his mom and dad speaking and looking at him. The three of them were standing with their wings around each other, looking at the breathtakingly beautiful crimson sunset.

Once more the question was asked: "Who loves you, honey?"

Karl paused for a moment then whispered, with his beak trembling, "The Navigator?"

"Yes, he does, son," said his dad.

"He loves everyone," Mom added.

Karl, surprised, gaped at his mom and dad. "You know him, too?"

"Yes, for many years, even before you were born."

"Mom, Dad why ..." he stopped, swallowed hard and sighed, "Why didn't you come and see me at flight school? Why did you leave me all alone?"

"Son, we tried to get back to you many times, but each time we were turned away by storms. One was a hurricane. We were carried so far off course by that one that we found ourselves on an unknown island. We were really lost. Mom got hurt. We stayed there for months until she recovered. Then it took us a very long time to find our way back to the flight school. When we did arrive, we were brokenhearted to hear what had happened, and to know that you had run away."

His mom began to cry. Dad reached out, pulled her close, and held her trembling body.

Instantly Karl remembered the Navigator's words and the picture he saw in the pool of water. "I'm so sorry, Mom, Dad."

"Crack!" He bolted upright to find the Navigator placing wood onto the fire.

"Bad dream?" the Navigator inquired. Only he and Karl were awake.

"No, not really," he said, scratching his head and yawning, he walked over to him. "It was an interesting dream. I was with my mom and dad. We spoke about you." He turned and looked into the Navigator's eyes.

"Me?"

"Yes. Do you know my mom and dad?"

"Yes. They are wonderful parents."

"The dream confirmed what you told me. They really are looking for me."

"That's right, they still are."

"Will I ever see them again?"

"In time, in time. You should lie back down and finish your sleep, it's still quite late. In the morning everyone will be waking up to a new day of adventures."

"Alright," Karl yawned and leaning against the Navigator, fell back to sleep. The Navigator just smiled and gently laying Karl's head on his lap, began to stroke his feathers, and softly sang:

"You are loved, you are loved.

Forever in my heart, you are loved.

No one will ever take your place

 Where you are in my heart

For you are loved, you are loved.

Forever in my heart you are loved."

Then he whispered, "You are loved."

Karl sighed. The Navigator looked into the sky and said to the Creator, "You've made this one especially wonderful." A tear caressed his cheek with great thankfulness for the moment.

CHAPTER 29

AN APPROACHING STORM

B efore dawn the temperature dramatically dropped, and a strong wind began to blow, awakening the crew around the long dead campfire.

"I'm cold," shivered Chloe, trying to snuggle closer under Lovely's wing.

Alby was looking toward the horizon, not able to see much because sunrise was still hours away.

"Look!" shouted Seaworthy as lightning struck the water, with thunder so heavy it shook the ground.

Alby gathered everyone together. "We've got to get into the cave at the Cove of Abandonment."

"No! I can't go back there!" Karl cried.

"It's the only place we'll be safe. This storm is too strong for us," Alby encouraged.

Chloe called out softly, her voice fading into the wind as it continued growing even stronger, "Please come with us."

"We'll protect you," said Schraeder.

"You don't understand!" shouted Karl, shaking with fear.

BANG!!! Thunder announced the storm's arrival on the island.

"You don't know what went on there!" tearfully shuddered Karl.

Behind him, he heard the Navigator's voice, "You must go back and face your fear, for that which sought to hold you captive has no hold on you any longer. It is only the memory that haunts you. There is nothing there to harm you any more."

"Quick now," the Navigator continued to everyone. "Karl, I will take care of Schraeder and Salty. Everyone else to the Cove! We'll meet you there."

Alby picked up Shelby, Chloe buried herself under Lovely's feathers, and they took off for the cove with Seaworthy leading the way.

BANG!!! Crack! Lightning hit the tree they had camped under, nearly splitting it in half. Fire blazed from it, catching the dry grass on fire. The wind blew it into a swirling frenzy of red and yellow flames, creating a diabolical dance.

"Hurry! We've got no time to waste!" the Navigator urged.

One by one they left the mountain. Salty and Schraeder ran to the Navigator. He picked them up and ran with Karl toward a secluded passage between two gigantic boulders, covered by brush and partially buried. The Navigator and Karl quickly situated Salty and Schraeder behind the rocks even as they cleared away the dead vegetation. The fire was racing toward the cove, completely out of control. There was no sense to the speed with which it moved changing direction as if orchestrated by a feverish conductor.

Another lightning bolt appeared, and then another so bold that it seemed to make the island glow in the night sky.

"Navigator, I'm scared, "cried Salty. Schraeder couldn't talk, he just kept nodding his head in agreement. Another lightning bolt came, startling them again.

"Ah, there it is," said the Navigator, pushing back the last bushes, revealing a small but thick wooden door, covered in moss.

"Navigator, please hurry! The fire is getting closer," screamed Salty.

"Karl, I need you to fly back and make sure everyone is safe and accounted for. We'll be ok. Trust me."

As Karl flew away, he glanced back and saw the flames had almost reached the Navigator, who had picked up Salty and Schraeder.

Swiftly, the Navigator kicked the door open, leaving it dangling by a single hinge. Hurrying, they crawled under the precariously hanging door into a passageway. They were safe but where were they?

Salty and Schraeder looked at the Navigator, grateful for their rescue, and feeling a calm assurance that they were safe with him, no matter where they were.

Chapter 30

Injured

"Where should we go?" asked Seaworthy, as they landed safely at the Cove.

"BANG!" Another lightning bolt struck a couple of trees behind them, flinging flaming chunks of wood and branches into the air.

Alby directed everyone into the cave. Following a channel of water, it led them to a vast open room. Big enough for ships to hide out. Everyone entered cautiously, but Karl stayed outside, staring with wide-eyed fear. Memories came flooding back.

"I can't..." he whispered

The fire continued to the shore, devouring everything in its path. Smoke began to enter the cave.

Alby bravely went to the mouth of the cave and tried to coax Karl to come inside, away from the heat of the flames edging ever so near. Sparks began to drift down, the intense wind bringing the fire closer and closer.

"You've got to get inside, Karl. We're family. We all need you. Come on. Let's go!" Alby encouraged with a tender wing around him.

Chloe flew out to meet Karl. "Quick, Karl, you're in danger! I don't want to see you get hurt. You're my friend." She began to cough from the smoke and then, "Ow!" She cried out in pain. A spark burned one of her wings, knocking her right to the ground. She lay unconscious.

"Chloe!" Karl shouted out. He immediately forgot all of his fears and the oncoming danger. Rushing to Chloe's side, he scooped her up and ran into the cave, Alby following close behind. Karl ran past their friends to a corner where he remembered there was fresh water trickling into a small rock basin. He laid Chloe next to the water. The gentle water spray gradually revived Chloe, but the damage was done to her wing. She could no longer fly. Karl noticed the injury and turned away to weep silently. Their friends all rushed to him and Chloe.

Karl held back the tears to fondly look at her and said: "...but you were born to fly." He could no longer contain his emotions. He fell into Alby's wings and wept uncontrollably.

"Chloe, are you ok?" asked Lovely, gently picking her up and holding her on her soft feathered lap.

BANG! CRACK! Two flaming trees fell across the opening to the cave, blocking their way out, a strong reminder that the storm and the fire were still alive, not willing to yield their destructive forces. The heat intensified as the smoke continued billowing into the cave. Everyone began coughing.

"Are you all ok?" A familiar voice called out into the dark smoke-filled cave. It was the Navigator, coming down the hidden passageway with Salty and Schraeder in tow.

"Navigator, it's Chloe; she got hurt really bad," sobbed Karl.

The Navigator made his way over to Chloe and saw she was breathing hard. "Karl, come with me quickly. Hurry, we can't waste any time."

More and more coughing could be heard as they left together. "There's a door back up there where Salty and Schraeder came down. If we can get that door off its hinge, we can create a wind tunnel to blow out the smoke. If we can't, someone could die."

"Is Chloe going to die?" asked Karl.

"Are you coming, Schraeder?"

Footsteps could be heard behind them, it was Schraeder, hustling to catch up. "Right behind you."

CHAPTER 31

FIRE AND RAIN

"Salty, come here and help me with Chloe," called Lovely. "Dip your paw in the water and touch her head lightly." She did. "Now touch her burned wing with some drops of water to ease the pain."

"Chloe, does that feel better?"

Chloe responded weakly, "Yes," with no further words.

Shelby got into the water to see what damage had been done to the channel while the tree burned above him. It was a dangerous expedition, but he wanted to be sure there was a chance for a safe exit if needed.

Chloe drifted in and out of consciousness. Her wound was serious and started looking infected.

"Will she ever fly again?" Salty asked Lovely.

"I don't know."

Meanwhile the Navigator, Karl, and Schraeder reached the door, which was partially ablaze. Karl and Schraeder struggled to see how to get the door off its heavily charred hinge without getting burned.

The heat was almost intolerable. Flames were still consuming trees and the heavy vegetation outside.

Karl noticed the wind had suddenly changed direction, "Quick! Here's our chance." Karl ran ahead of the Navigator and slammed his body into the door. Schraeder couldn't do anything to help, for the heat was overwhelming him. Karl's effort didn't yield the intended outcome.

"HELP!" One of Karl's wings was hit with fiery debris! Schraeder noticed some moss on the floor untouched by the flames. Karl fell onto the floor of the passageway, trying to roll out the fire. At the same time Schraeder grabbed some of the moss and wrapped it on Karl's wing, suffocating the smoldering embers.

Suddenly the Navigator came alongside Karl, shielding him from the flames just beyond the doorway. The wind had changed direction yet again.

In pain, Karl said, "We've got to get that door off." He spied a large rock. It took all three of them to pick it up and to thrust it against the door. THUD!

A little movement, but no success. The rock rolled down a ways behind them. Again, they picked it up, Karl grunting, "One more tiiime!"

Schraeder spoke up, "Let's aim at that bolt that's sticking out a little at the bottom."

"Good idea," said the Navigator.

"Here we goooo! One, Two, Threeeee!"

The rock slammed just a little off the mark but the door did move a bit.

"I think we need to do it once more," said Karl, wincing in pain.

"How's your wing?" asked the Navigator.

"Haven't got time to worry about that. The family needs us. They've got to get fresh air and we're running out of time."

"I'm with you, Karl," said the Navigator.

"Me too," added Schraeder.

They gathered around the rock one more time, trying to lift it higher than before when a strong gust of wind struck the door so forcefully it blew out the flames and knocked the door completely off the hinge! The door rattled against boulders and then 'poof!' it was gone in the blink of an eye.

Karl looked at the Navigator, while Schraeder just stared outside to see where the door went.

"Well, that was easy," joked Schraeder.

They all chuckled. Then drip......drip.....drip, drip, drip, it started to rain. The wind had become so blustery that it shoved them them down the slippery passageway. The fresh air had arrived!

"Hear that, feel that?" said Alby. Everyone inside the cave was still fighting the smoke.

The wind blew out all the smoke, and the rain transformed into a torrential downpour. The fire and the flaming trees blocking their exit were being extinguished, and the smoke was carried out over the sea.

"Oh, that feels so good." said Salty.

As the wind howled its way through the cave, a faint sound could be heard, becoming louder and louder. "Whoa!!!" It was the Navigator with Karl and Schraeder. They slid down the tunnel, looping up one side of the walls and then down the other, turning them around several times and then Splat! They landed in a pile of mud. The rain water had soaked into all the dirt, making it into a slippery mess.

Karl rushed to Chloe's side, shaking the moss from his injured wing. It was sore, but he didn't let on, for he was more concerned for his friend. "How is she?" he asked.

"She hasn't spoken in a while. She's breathing better now," said Lovely as she gently nuzzled Chloe's little face with her beak.

"What do you think, Navigator? You can do anything," said Salty.

Shelby emerged from his underwater expedition, and saw Karl's wound. "Here, let me put this on your wing. It's a paste I made from the sediment in the channel. This should take away some of the pain and keep it from getting infected." He carefully applied it. Though Karl didn't appreciate the attention, he graciously accepted Shelby's kindness.

The rain continued. Though the thunder and lightning had ceased, the rain became a deluge, quenching the rampant fires. Although one problem was gone, another became clear.

The water began pouring in from the open doorway, settling in the cave.

The group decided they needed to get to higher ground. The floodwaters enabled Fairhaven to move closer to rescue his friends.

"Fairhaven? What? How?"

"It's ok, Karl. I've come to tell you that you can trust the Navigator. Listen to him and one day we will see each other again."

"Fairhaven....? It was only a dream," Karl muttered as he turned over and went back to sleep.

The campfire was still gently warming them all, though burning down to a few glowing embers.

CHAPTER 32

JEALOUSY

In the morning they awakened to a crisp, clear sunrise. Great cumulus clouds began to form.

"Wow! It's so beautiful!" said Seaworthy.

All day long Karl couldn't shake the dream, 'What did it mean?'

Back at the beach, Shelby was having a discouraging day. He felt neglected by the group, and that Karl was getting all the attention. He started thinking thoughts that were not true of himself.

"If I only had two claws, maybe the Navigator would love me. I'm so different than everybody else. I can't even fly." He slowly crawled away, isolating himself from his friends. He sulked the rest of the day as if he had a cloud of gloom and despair over his head.

Walter was swimming by and noticed Shelby was looking out of sorts. He got out of the water and shuffled to Shelby's home. With a tap of his tusk on the shell, "Hey, little guy. Why so glum?"

"Nobody's home, go away. Can't you read the sign?"

"What sign?"

A claw emerged from the shell and scrawled in the sand. 'Go Away!' A muffled sound came from his shell, "that sign," pointing to it.

Silence.

Only the ocean's waves could be heard. Shelby peeked out with one eye. Seeing it was Walter, he said "Oh, it's you." Then he turned his shell away from Walter.

Walter frowned and gently flipped Shelby up into the air, hooked the entrance of his shell, and returned to the Sea of Life with him.

Shelby shrieked, "Help! What are you doing?"

Walter began floating on his back and deposited Shelby onto his belly. "Shelby, what's wrong? We're out here a ways and no one can hear us. You don't seem like yourself today."

Shelby sighed and said, "Everyone's so enthralled with Karl this and Karl that. I'm sick of it. What about me? I hurt too. I'm lonely. Doesn't anyone care how I feel?"

"Shelby, are you jealous of all the attention Karl's getting?"

"Who? Me? I don't think so. But the Navigator spends so much time with Karl and he hardly ever talks with me. I guess he likes Karl more than me." He sighed. "I like Karl, too; but I really wish the Navigator wanted to spend time with me once in a while."

"Shelby," Walter began, "if the Navigator didn't care about you, why would he have given you such a wonderful family of friends?"

"They're not my family. They're not like me and I'm not like them. I'm different. I don't fit in." Shelby sighed an even deeper sigh.

"Don't look at what you don't have. Recognize what you do have and how unique you are to the importance of this family. Be grateful. I don't have two legs and I shuffle. You can crawl. We both get around and we get along with each other in spite of our differences. No one is exactly the same as anyone else. We are each uniquely made, each one has a value and a role to play in life. What is yours? What is mine? Maybe mine right now is to be reaching out to you as a friend to tell you I value your friendship, and the Navigator certainly values yours, too.

"You value me... as a friend?"

"Yes, I do."

A tear rolled down Shelby's face, dropping onto his claw. He held it up to the sunlight. It glistened then it fell, blending into the sea.

"Thanks, Walter. Maybe you're right. If I look to help others, maybe I'll be less focused on myself."

"You would be missed if anything ever happened to you."

In the distance, voices were calling out his name.

"Shelby, are you coming?" Seaworthy called out. "The Navigator wants us to get together with him."

"He said he won't start till Shelby shows up," said Karl.

"Really?" Shelby asked as they returned to the shore.

"Yeah. Let's go, Shelby." Seaworthy spoke as he scooped him up. "Walter, you and Gwen are invited, too." Then he hurried back to the Cove.

"I'll get Gwen and we'll meet you there," shouted Walter as he went back into the water.

"Hey, you!" A charming voice called out to Walter. "Where are you going?" It was Gwen.

"Hi, sweetheart," Walter began, "The Navigat...."

"I know," she interrupted. "Let's go. Schraeder and Salty came over and told me we were invited."

"Yes, we did." Salty and Schraeder were getting a free ride on Gwen's back. As Walter came closer, Schraeder made a run for it.

"Here I come, Walter!" He grabbed hold of Walter's whiskers.

"Oww!"

"Oops, sorry about that."

When everyone had arrived, the Navigator welcomed them, then sat down and began to share wonderful stories of the Creator and his great love for each of them.

"I remember one time a young fledgling, a beautiful bird came to me and said, 'I don't know how to sing.'

"Song birds learn to sing in the dark," I told her. She seemed a little embarrassed. "Why don't you sing?" I asked.

"No one ever taught me." She turned her head away from me.

"I'll teach you," I told her.

"I'd like that. Why is it so dark when we learn to sing?"

"So you can focus on what you're doing with no distractions. This gets you ready for the stage light at dawn."

"Stage light?"

"Look!" I pointed to the horizon, the morning sunrise. "That's the stage light and that's when you'll sing your little heart out. Let your song go forth with all that's within you. Your song will be a song of joy, a song declaring a new day of hope is arising. The lessons learned in the darkness prepare you for the light."

Once again the time spent with the Navigator made it seem like time stood still, for each story was so amazing they all wanted another and another.

In the afternoon when the Navigator was getting ready to leave, Shelby bashfully came up to him and said, "Navigator, thank you for calling for me to join you today."

"Shelby, you are very special to me."

"Me? Really? Why?"

"I have no one else like you in the whole world, that's what makes you so special to me and to each one of your family here. You are uniquely made, you are a delight to me each time we're together."

"But, I only have one claw...and I can't fly."

"Oh, Shelby, that doesn't matter to me. I'd love you just as much if you had three claws."

"Now that would be weird," Seaworthy said, adding, "Where would you put the third one?"

Shelby smirked with a wrinkled brow looking at the Navigator. They both began to laugh.

The Navigator added, "I suppose you're right." The Navigator picked up Shelby and said, "Shelby, I have always loved you and will forever love you and you know what?"

"What?"

"You are a lot of fun to be with. Shelby, go back and join your family. Don't let your differences pull you away from them. Know that you add significance to the whole family. They are not complete without you. Like a missing puzzle piece, you help bring the whole picture together. I will see you again."

Chapter 33

The Slide

"Whee!" The sound of excitement broke the silence. "This is fantastic, Karl!" exclaimed Seaworthy.

They had located the old slide. It had been hidden behind dead vines. When they had finished removing the overgrowth, they climbed on board and off they went! It was a very long downhill ride with a number of surprise twists and turns.

Thud! Oof!

They collided at the finish line, laughing and falling over each other, and getting a few bruises.

"Let's do it again!" Seaworthy said.

A loud roar and a scream of joy rose from behind them. Coming rapidly down the slide was Alby. "Whoooa!" Thud! He bowled over both Seaworthy and Karl. They were too slow in getting out of the way. All three shared a laugh. Everyone else rushed over to see what the excitement was all about.

"You found it!" smiled Alby. "I used to ride this with the Navigator when I was much younger. We had so much fun on this," moving his wing over the edge of the slide, giving it a few hardy taps like encountering an old friend not seen in a very long time.

"I want to go," said Schraeder.

"Me too," said Salty, hesitantly.

"It's a ways up there," said Alby.

"Come on, we'll get you up there," said Karl. "Alby, I'll get Schraeder. You get Salty."

"Shelby, you coming?" asked Alby.

"I'll get him," said Seaworthy. Before Shelby could respond, only two words could be heard as they flew off, "OoooooOH, Nooooooooo!"

They all landed safely high on the hill overlooking the cove.

"Wow! What a view!" said Schraeder.

"Shelby, ready?"

"Ah, can we discuss this first?" asked Shelby.

"Too late!" said Seaworthy, screaming with excitement. Just then an unexpected guest jumped on board behind them as well.

"Karl!"

Schraeder was on the sidelines watching this all take place and had an idea. He quickly got some palm branches and began to peel away the leaves and started weaving something.

"What are those? They look like slippers," said Salty.

"I'm calling them sliders." After securing them to his feet with a green vine, he proceeded to climb onto the slide. He tried to stand up but began slipping and sliding. "Well, here goes nothing."

With a leap forward, whoosh! He was on his way. He was sliding down standing up, but once in a while he was swirling up one side and then the other. Surprisingly he caught up to Karl, Seaworthy and Shelby.

"Coming through!" Schraeder shouted. He jumped up in the air and landed in front of them.

"Wow! That was cool!" said Karl.

The shock of Schraeder's appearance caused Seaworthy, who was holding Shelby, to throw up his wings and accidentally release Shelby into the stratosphere. He landed back at the top of the slide, teetering on the edge of it. Shelby sighed just a big enough sigh to topple onto the slide and career down faster and faster.

Schraeder, already at the end of the slide, hadn't thought about how he would stop. Because he was so light, he flew into the air and was surprised to be caught by...Lovely, who was flying by and saw Schraeder needed a soft place to land. She caught him in mid-air, landing just as Karl and Seaworthy came off the slide.

"Wow! That was great! I want to do it again!" Seaworthy flew back to the start when he heard, "I told them I didn't want to go in the first place. Crustaceons are not supposed to sli-yi—yi-de!"

He looked down the slide and realized somehow they had lost Shelby. Shelby was tumbling over and over, causing the sand in his shell to fly all over the place.

"I'm coming!" shouted Seaworthy, heading to the rescue. He grabbed some of Schraeder's leftover palm leaves, wrapped them around his butt, hopped on the slide, and gained speed like a fine waxed toboggan.

"Hold on, ol' buddy. I'm almost there!" Shelby was still screaming.

"I gotcha," Seaworthy said, trying to pick up Shelby. But then Seaworthy began screaming. The palm leaves had wrapped around his face, and he was sliding down with no cushion, causing friction to his back side. He thought he saw smoke coming from the slide, but it was him.

Still screaming, he forgot about Shelby, bumping him and sending him into orbit. Thud! Seaworthy hit the ground running and jumped into the water. "Aahhh!" The cool water was a welcome relief.

Shelby was still yelling as he stuck his head out of his shell, glasses crooked, and his eyes rolling around like pinwheels in a brisk wind.

"Tell me this is fun, right?" He collapsed into his shell just as he plunged into the sea. Only bubbles could be seen from where he sank.

Everyone rushed to the shore looking for Shelby. All that could be seen were bubbles slowly approaching them. A creature emerged covered in seaweed.

"Shelby, you ok?" Seaworthy paused and added. "Want to go again?" he asked, still pumped with the adrenaline high.

Shelby stood up, arched his back and keeled over. "No comment."

"Want some help?" Chloe came by and began to sneeze. Shelby reached his claw to stop her.

"Oh, don't you dare sneeze now! I want to stay mad at him. You, YOU!" pointing his claw and staring at Seaworthy.

"You said you were having fun. Right?" questioned Seaworthy, gently trying to sit down.

"Achoo!" Chloe did it again, with a rainbow of colors affecting everyone.

Shelby gave up being angry and admitted, "Yes, it was fun...but only a little."

Everyone laughed. Seaworthy picked up Shelby and began tossing him into the air, with one friend after another tossing him back and forth while singing, "For he's a jolly good fellow..."

When they stopped, Shelby wobbled from dizziness, plopped over and said groggily, "I think... I need... a nap."

Chapter 34

A Familiar Place

Early the next day Seaworthy and Karl thought they would climb up the hilly terrain to the mountain summit to see what was beyond the Cove.

"You know, Seaworthy, this looks so familiar to me, like I've been here before. I don't know why," mused Karl.

"You've been here before and never told us? This is beautiful," added Seaworthy.

They had arrived at the mountain peak, and saw a view that took their breath away.

"We've got to tell the others about this. This is too wonderful to keep to ourselves."

"I agree," said Seaworthy. "But let's keep walking and see what other discoveries we find before heading back."

Karl walked away from Seaworthy to study a strange rock formation partly covered by overgrowth. As he peeled back some of the brush, he found an old wooden door. "This looks so familiar. I don't understan...."

His thought was interrupted when Seaworthy called out "Let's bring everybody up here to see this place."

"Sounds good to me," agreed Karl. They decided to fly back with the news of their discovery.

All the while Karl wracked his brain; "Where have I seen this before?"

"Race you," called Seaworthy as he suddenly took off.

"Hey!" Karl flew off, trailing behind him only by a few yards.

Seaworthy arrived first and Karl settled for second place.

"Hey everybody, come here. Seaworthy and I have something to tell you."

"What is it?" asked Shelby.

"Yes, tell us, tell us," said Chloe, excitedly.

Salty and Schraeder arrived with Alby and Lovely.

"We found a beautiful view of the Sea of Life. There's a green meadow nestled between large rock formations up there." Karl pointed it out.

"We want you to come with us and see it," added Seaworthy.

They all made plans to go there to see the view.

CHAPTER 35

GATHERING ON THE MOUNTAIN TOP

It was only a few hours before sunset when everyone gathered to go up the mountain to see the breathtaking view Seaworthy and Karl had described. Plans had been made to start a fire and enjoy the evening sky as the stars appeared at twilight. A slight breeze blew and a chill filled the air.

"We should be going soon," said Chloe. "I can't fly when it's windy. I get off course very easily."

"Everyone follow me," said Karl.

Seaworthy called out, "Follow me first." Off he went laughing, thinking he was the leader. Karl just shrugged his shoulders, not caring who led the way.

Alby questioned Shelby, "Are you coming? You can ride with me."

"No, I've had enough high flying excitement for today."

"Ok, see you later," said Alby.

Lovely was about to leave with Alby when she noticed she hadn't seen Chloe leave. "Chloe, where are you?"

"Over here," she sighed, huffing and puffing, flapping her little wings furiously. She wasn't getting anywhere as the breeze began to pick up a little more.

"Why don't we fly together? Here, curl up under my wing and you'll be fine."

"Oh, this is much better, even warmer with your feathers around me. Thanks."

"Shelby, I can come back and get you. Are you sure you don't want to come?" asked Lovely.

"No, thank you, Lovely. I'm going to visit Walter and Gwendolyn in the morning. I plan on sharing another one of my illustrious adventures on the Sea of Life," he replied.

"Ok, see you tomorrow."

CHAPTER 36

A FIRE, A STORM, A DREAM?

After arriving, Schraeder got busy.

"What a great fire! This is perfect for a night of looking at the stars," said Salty, greatly impressed with one of Schraeder's hidden talents. Everyone agreed that the fire was spectacular and --- warm.

The stars began to emerge from the darkness. Then the moon appeared and reflected off the sea, its gentle waves being the only sound besides the fire's crackling embers as the sparks rose and dissolved into the night sky. Hours went by, and one by one they drifted off to sleep. Late into the evening a low rumbling could be heard in the far off distance.

Only Alby noticed it first. Rising, he went to the cliff overlooking the sea and observed lightning. The wind began to pick up a little, thunder came closer.

Seaworthy slowly opened his eyes and noticed Alby in the moonlight looking out at the sea. The fire had become a bed of coals, the wind occasionally fanning it to flame, but dying down again.

"Alby, everything alright?"

"Not sure. That storm looks like it's headed right toward us."

"BOOM!" Lightning cracked loudly, startling everyone. The wind began to groan in a deep howling tone.

"I'm sc-sc-sc-scared!" shivered Chloe, burrowing her body into Lovely's wing. "I can't fly in this strong wind," she added, lifting her head to look at Lovely.

Alby ran back with Seaworthy and told everyone: "Quick! Everyone, get back to the Cove, right now!"

"BOOM!" Another bolt of lightning cracked not far from where they sat. They could feel the earth rumbling underneath them.

"Hurry, that storm is almost upon us."

Lovely stretched out her wing, inviting Chloe in for a safe ride. Off they went, mistakenly leaving Salty and Schraeder behind.

"What about us?" yelled Salty.

Their plea for help was drowned out by another "BOOM!" It made Salty jump into Schraeder's arms, causing Schraeder to stagger around, trying to keep his balance.

Shelby, meanwhile, was asleep on the beach in his cozy home dreaming marvelous dreams when little by little the waves began to reach his spot on the beach. Each wave drew closer and closer toward his home. Then, "CRASH!" a huge wave smashed against his home, awaking Shelby,"Who? What?"

Before he could finish his thought, another wave crashed over him, dragging him back into the sea.

"Whoa!" he yelled. He stuck his head out to see what was happening, only to see a huge wave heading right for him.

"Uh, oh," he sighed. The wave pushed him back into his home with a flood of water. "Help! Help!" he gurgled, gagging on it.

A familiar voice came loud and clear. "Hey, little guy, I got you." It was Walter. He hooked Shelby's home with one of his tusks and swam hard against the current, bringing him to the safety of the Cove.

"Thanks, Walter," said Shelby.

"You'll be safe here. There's a cave, get the others inside. They're already here at the Cove. Gwen and I will see you after this storm passes." Walter swam back out to her, fighting the growing swells and white caps.

"You ok?"

"Yeah, just a bit water logged. Walter says there's a cave – let's get everyone in it."

Shelby's stride had a noticeable swagger, like a big soaked diaper swinging from side to side. As funny as it looked, no one said a word. They were just glad to have Shelby back with them safe and sound.

Inside the cave, Chloe, who had injured her wing from the bonfire sparks, asked: "Where's Karl?"

"I don't know," said Lovely, "I thought he was right behind us."

"And where are Salty and Schraeder? I hope they're not stuck up on the mountain," said Seaworthy, looking this way and that as he peeked his head out of the cave.

"BANG!" Meanwhile back on the mountain, lightning struck the tree where they had all been only a short time ago. The tree split in two, caught fire and ignited the dead vegetation, consuming everything in its path.

Salty and Schraeder were scurrying away from the tree when Karl returned to rescue them. Schraeder said, "Boy, are we glad to see you!" Salty agreed.

"I could fly one of you out right now," Karl stated, "but the other may not make it till I get back."

The winds grew stronger and the flames jumped from tree to tree, spreading rapidly through the brush.

"We've got to do something!" shouted Salty. The heat was growing and she was afraid her fur might catch on fire.

They tried to run back toward the trail they had taken to come up in the first place, but the winds changed direction and flames cut off that option.

Then Karl remembered his dream. "That's it! Quick, follow me!" They ran to a large rock formation covered with dry brush and decaying vines. "Help me get these off of this rock wall! I know there's a door here somewhere!"

Salty and Schraeder looked puzzled. Turning to each other, they said, "A door???"

They thrashed through the debris as fast as they could, all the while the flames crawled closer.

"BANG!" Another lightning bolt struck, hitting the rock formation itself, sending granite tumbling down, startling them.

"Aha! I knew it was here." Karl found the door, just as he pictured it.

"How did you know it was here?" asked Schraeder.

"It's probably a long story, right?" said Salty sarcastically, and quipped, "We got a little problem here." She pointed to the approaching flames.

"It will be a good story, if we get out of this," said Karl, still removing debris. Finally, their work paid off and the door handle became visible. Karl tried to pull on it, but it wouldn't budge. They each took turns with no success. Fear came over them. Panicking, they screamed out for the Navigator.

"Don't you see us? Fairhaven always told us he felt that someone was watching over him. You told us the Creator sees us. Navigator, please come and help us. We're going to die!" Salty cried out.

Karl spoke up and said, "I have this feeling we're going to be ok."

Salty was sweating profusely.

"Karl, look at Salty. She doesn't look so good," Schraeder observed.

Suddenly she passed out, crumbling to the ground. They pulled her away from the flames, moving her from the door to a cleft in the rocks. She started to come to.

"Look!" Schraeder said, "Here's a big rock we can use as a hammer."

"You stay here," said Karl, speaking to Salty.

"Ok, but it's so hot."

"Schraeder, let me help you carry that rock," Karl said.

They knew they had to work fast. Karl picked up the rock and began banging it as hard as he could against the door handle. No movement. They tried again. Nothing.

Schraeder noticed one of the hinges was broken. "Karl, hit the hinge here on the bottom, maybe that will get the door loosened up."

On the third try, the hinge finally lost its grip. They found a little edge and tried to pull the door to the side. They kept pulling and pushing it, then a shrill squeak and grating sound. The door had budged, but only a few inches; it was digging into the ground.

Just then a heavy burst of wind blew against them as they struggled to free the door. The door moved a couple of feet, releasing cool air that pushed back the flames that were only a few feet away.

"Quick, let's grab Salty. I think we can squeeze through the opening."

"I've got her." It was the Navigator; he had been protecting Salty the whole time from the flames and now carried her in his arms.

"Let's go!" said Schraeder. "Navigator, get Salty in there first."

Getting down on his knees with Salty, the Navigator was able to get her in safely by crawling in on his back.

"Karl, you're next."

"Schraeder, you should…"

"No time to argue, get going."

After Karl got in, they waited for Schraeder. No Schraeder appeared.

Karl got on his knees and called out through the doorway "Schraeder! SCHRAEDER!!!"

"Where is he?" asked a weak Salty.

"Navigator, watch over Salty, I've got to go back and get Schraeder."

The door was getting hot and Karl singed a wing, but managed to get out and found Schraeder curled up in a ball not far from the entrance. The smoke had gotten so thick, he had lost his bearings and was coughing violently when Karl caught up to him.

Karl quickly lifted him into a fireman's carry, got back to the door; and the Navigator pulled them both into safety. Karl's wing was smoldering; obviously he was burned and in pain. The Navigator grabbed some moss and put it on his wing, easing the pain and stopping the burning.

Schraeder's coughing eventually stopped as he breathed in the cool air.

At least they were safe for now in the tunnel that led to an unknown destination.

They waited a bit to allow Salty, Karl and Schraeder to gain back their strength. When everyone was ready, they began their journey down the dark, dank corridor.

Chapter 37

Mud Slide

"**B**OOM!" The loud clap of thunder was followed by a cloudburst. Rain poured down so heavily that it began to put out the fire, but also caused a mud flow making its way slowly down the sides of the mountain.

As the rain poured down, the mud covered the mossy steps.

"Whoa!!!" Salty lost her footing while following too closely behind Karl and Schraeder, causing them to fall down like bowling pins, one fell upon the other and down they tumbled.

"THUD! OOH! YIIE!"

They had abruptly arrived at the bottom of the stairs. Slowly they sorted out whose arm was whose and whose foot was where. They finally stood up, stretched, and brushed themselves off. Turning around to see where they were, they found themselves not lost at all but with their traveling companions. The family was finally together again.

Alby and Seaworthy rushed over to them, tightly hugged them, and breathed a sigh of relief for their safe return. Shelby waved his claw welcoming them, "Glad you're back with us."

Inside the cave they heard an eerie sound.

Seaworthy made his way outside to look around and found all the ground had become a thick gooey muck. A sucking sound happened each time he struggled to pull his foot out. The mud was at least 5 inches deep, and getting deeper. Then the unexpected happened.

"I'm stuck," he sighed.

The eerie sound continued, everyone froze and listened. The sound was coming from above. The mountain began to shake.

"What is that?" quavered Salty.

"Swoosh!!!" The sound was deafening.

"Mud slide!" yelled Alby. He had flown out to find the source of the sound. "You are all safer to stay in the cave."

"Let's hope the Navigator comes to help us soon," said Shelby.

"I'm sure he's not far away," softly whispered Chloe. Lovely held Chloe close to her body because Chloe had begun to shiver again.

"Uncle Alby, help me!" screamed Seaworthy.

As Alby flew to the rescue, he shouted out again, "Quick! Everyone get back into the cave!"

Mud began sealing the opening of the cave. Everyone turned and ran deeper inside

When Alby reached Seaworthy, he saw a river of mud oozing toward him. There was only a small moment of time to get him out. If he couldn't get Seaworthy free, he would be buried alive.

"Seaworthy, grab my feet and hold on while I flap my wings. Try to pick your feet up."

"I can't!"

"Try again!" Alby continued flapping his wings even harder.

As the mud creeped closer, the massive wall pushed everything out of its way. A large boulder and a tree were coming toward him, when the tree was stopped by the boulder. They settled right next to Seaworthy.

"Seaworthy, try to push off from the tree." Alby rocked him back and forth. "Pop!" One foot got free. "Snap!" The tree broke free of the rock, bringing a pocket of air to the other foot, finally releasing it.

Seaworthy was free; filthy, but free. They flew back into the cave while dodging plopping clumps of mud still flowing from the mountain top.

"That was close."

"Sure was," gasped Alby as they both fell to the cave's floor in exhaustion.

"Thanks, Uncle Alby," Seaworthy panted.

"I would have stayed with you no matter what," Alby assured. Quite winded, he turned over and laid on his back.

Everyone breathed a huge sigh of relief.

Lovely was busy tending to Chloe who was not well; she had taken in too much smoke, and with the burns she received on her wings, she could no longer fly.

"How did you get here?" asked Alby.

"The Navigator got us out of danger," said Salty. "He saved my life."

"Where is he ?" asked Schraeder.

The Navigator was nowhere to be found.

"Chloe!" Karl shouted, remembering his dream. He pushed his way to her, gently putting his wing over her injured wing. Staring at her, he sighed, "Chloe."

She slowly opened her eyes and faintly smiled, "I knew you could do it."

"Do what?"

"Resc..." She coughed. And coughed, "Rescue Salty and Schraeder. You're my hero." She wheezed, coughing again.

"Me? Come on now, you need to rest. The Navigator will be here and he'll fix you up."

"It's ok, Karl, it's my time to go home with him." She spoke so weakly that Karl was alarmed.

"Home? Home is here with us. We're family."

"The Port of Heaven sounds so beautiful and peaceful there. Remember the Navigator's stories of the Creator? I'll even get to meet Fairhaven and perhaps Blanding."

Tears filled Karl's eyes.

"Karl, you were born for such a time as this. Without you..." she coughed again. "Salty and Schraeder would never have made it. You put yourself into the face of death to rescue the ones you love. That's a hero."

"But, Chloe, I couldn't rescue you, and you were born to fly. Remember?" His voice trailed off to a faint whisper while his beak began to quiver.

"Oh, but I did; and because of you I'm flying even higher than I ever could before. My heart is soaring way above my physical limitations. To see you finally finding forgiveness and recognizing you really are free. That makes my heart soar."

"There is no longer any stronghold or remnant of the bondage Cutter held over you," spoke the Navigator, walking into the cave, placing his hand on Karl's shoulder.

Karl turned and hugged the Navigator, pleading with him, "Can't you do something to help Chloe? Please! She's my friend."

"Karl, it's time for Chloe to come home with me to the Port of Heaven."

"But..." Karl ran out of words to say. The unbearable thought of losing Chloe was too much to imagine.

Chapter 38

An Old Friend Returns

The rain had stopped and the sun was breaking through the clouds.

"Ahoy!" came a shout from the inlet.

Karl stood motionless. It was a familiar voice. Could it be?... "No," he thought, "it's not possible."

Slowly Karl walked toward the voice, passing through his friends one by one.

"Ahoy!"

Pushing through the muddy debris, Karl left the cave.

"Brickwater," Karl whispered. He flew to meet Brickwater, landing on his bow. "I'm so sorry I said those words. I should never have done that to you. I didn't mean for you to die. It was all my fault." Karl sobbed uncontrollably while hugging his old friend.

"Karl, I never felt you were responsible. I've never held that thought in my heart against you. I made my own decision, a very bad one. At my lowest moment, a thought suddenly came to me: 'Remember the Navigator!'"

Karl wiped away his tears and said, "You knew the Navigator?"

"Yes, Karl, he had spoken to me many times, on the Sea of Life. I remembered him and I called on his name." Brickwater stopped to regain his composure, he was so overwhelmed by the memory of the Navigator's love for him.

He continued, "And he came when I needed him." Brickwater began to sob. "He picked up my broken pieces, and took me to the Port of Heaven, and made me whole."

Together they cried tears of joy and thankfulness for the Navigator's love.

"Brickwater, you look brand new."

"Yes, I am. I am not the same as I once was. I am whole."

Karl just shook his head with a big smile. He couldn't get over the change in Brickwater, knowing that he knew the Navigator and he too had been forgiven. Karl was overjoyed.

Brickwater spoke up, "Don't worry about Chloe. Yes, you will miss her, but she will be safe, well and happy with the Creator. You will always have a cherished memory of her that you will carry with you."

"By the way, why are you here?" asked Karl.

"To let you know where I am and that I forgive you. I'm also here to pick up the Navigator and Chloe."

All the others had come outside to watch the unfolding events. It was wonderful to experience Karl's release of the burden he had carried for so long. Everyone said their goodbyes to Chloe. Lovely had carried her to the water where the Navigator waited.

"It's time, Chloe."

"Ok." She sighed, "Can I say goodbye to my friend Karl?"

"Of course."

The Navigator and Chloe went to Brickwater.

Karl walked over to his dear friend and touched her injured wing gently. "Chloe, I am sure going to miss you but you are in really good hands now. You're still as cute and beautiful as the day we met."

"But I was a chubby little caterpillar," she replied.

"Maybe so, but you melted my heart that day. That day I realized I had a true friend. You will always be in my heart. I love you, Chloe."

Chloe smiled her biggest smile, sighed and with her last breath a rainbow of colors enveloped Karl and he no longer feared for Chloe. He smiled deeply and cried...Chloe was gone.

"She didn't sneeze?" Karl looked up at the Navigator while releasing her wing.

"She no longer has allergies. She has no more sickness, and all the pain is gone," said the Navigator.

Karl leaned his head on the Navigator, who kissed him.

"Karl, we need to go now. Go back to your family of friends, they are waiting for you."

"Thanks, Navigator...for everything. See you later, Brickwater."

"Yes, you will, someday," said Brickwater. "I'll be watching for you."

As Karl flew away the Navigator called out: "Karl, go back and find the shell that called out to you."

Karl turned around, puzzled, and saw that Brickwater, the Navigator and Chloe were gone.

CHAPTER 39

THE COVE OF SERENITY REVIVES

The family of friends had waved goodbye to the Navigator, Chloe and Brickwater. They looked around at the charred remains of the landscape. The cove's waters were filled with ashes, burnt twigs and logs, some still smoldering.

"What a mess!" It was Gwen and Walter.

"Ow!" Walter banged his head on a drifting log.

"What a storm!" exclaimed Gwen as they made their way onto the beach. "What's the matter?" added Gwen, seeing their downcast looks.

"Chloe died," softly responded Karl as he landed on the beach. Everyone else was silent.

"She was so sweet," said Gwen, starting to cry.

"Yes, and she was a fighter too," added Lovely.

Walter put his flipper around Gwen to comfort her. Lovely came over to her as well, with no words, just putting her head against Gwen's.

"Did you find the shell, Karl?" They all turned to see the Navigator walking down the beach toward them.

As the Navigator approached, something amazing began to happen. Wherever he walked, colors began to appear, and all the charred remains from the fire began to blow away. Bark began to grow back on the trees, leaves began to burst open. And flowers of every color began appearing. It was as if a divine paint brush made sweeping strokes of water colors. The Cove was completely restored! Everyone was in awe.

"This is for you," said the Navigator, extending his arms. "Karl, don't look back, the cave is as empty as if it had never been entered. There is no past to be remembered there, only the future yet to be written. Enjoy what I have done for you, for all of you."

"The fire burned out the old to usher in the new. This day I restore to you the Cove of Serenity, a place where joy and peace will exist."

As they walked down the beach with the Navigator:

Salty was amazed at the beautiful flowers, in such a colorful array.

Schraeder liked the movement of the tall grasses bending in the wind.

Seaworthy also enjoyed the breeze, as his feathers were fluffed.

Alby loved the sound of the waves washing upon the shore, engulfing his legs and feet.

Lovely appreciated the fresh salt air.

Shelby, well, he liked his, "zzz," nap.

Gwen and Walter loved each other and were grateful to be considered part of the family.

"This place looks beautiful. Remember, Alby?"

"It sure does, Professor."

The Professor had just arrived to check on everyone after he had weathered the storm at the Beacon of Hope Lighthouse.

"Professor, did you go to flight school with Alby?" asked Seaworthy.

"Yes, we were roommates," answered Alby as he began to reminisce with the Professor.

Seaworthy looked at everyone, and with a shrug, "It's a good school."

CHAPTER 40

A DREAM LIVES

A few days later, "Where are Salty and Schraeder?" asked the Professor.

No one knew. They had taken off earlier, wanting to reinspect the remains of the glider. They found the bent frame and a shredded wing flapping in the breeze, highly weather worn and sun bleached. Salty lifted up a piece of the lacerated wing, throwing it down in deep despair.

"What are we going to do, Schraeder?"

As they started to walk away, Seaworthy joined them. "The Professor is looking for you."

"Yeah, that's great, but we will never be able to get back to his home," sighed Schraeder.

The three continued silently walking. Seaworthy looked at them from time to time, wanting to say a word or two but saw that the best thing to do was to just be with them, figuring that sometimes the best thing to say is nothing at all.

Karl was visiting with Walter and Alby when the trio came around the bend in the shoreline. Gradually they ended their conversation as they turned their attention to Salty and Schraeder, sensing a deep sadness.

"Are you ok?" asked Karl, concerned.

"The Professor's glider is destroyed," explained Seaworthy.

Salty and Schraeder nodded their heads.

"And how will we ever get back home to the Beacon of Hope Lighthouse?" Salty felt defeated.

"What you need to do is to talk to the Navigator. Fairhaven used to do that a lot and he always helped him," encouraged Alby.

"But where is he?" they asked.

"We need him now!" cried Salty.

"I don't know, but he's never far away," said Alby.

"Navigator, please come and help us," earnestly pleaded Schraeder.

"Where are you, Navigator, now that we need you?" Salty wept.

No response.

"Do you want me to stay with you?" asked Seaworthy.

"Thanks, but we need to be alone right now."

They left their friends, agreeing that calling on the Navigator was the best thing they could do, believing he would hear their quiet desperation.

A ways further Salty and Schraeder saw a tree unusually close to the water. As they walked around it:

"Hello. I heard you calling my name. I told you I'll always be here for you."

It was the Navigator. He was sitting with his back resting against the tree, drawing in the sand with a stick. He stood, gathering Salty and Schraeder into his arms, and swirled around with them among the tall grass and cattails. The twirling turned into a dance, and the Navigator sang to them. Their despair faded away and hope emerged.

"Come, let's sit down together and rest a while." They laid their heads down on the Navigator's lap. He stroked the back of their heads and said softly, "Everything's going to be alright."

A quiet assurance enveloped them.

Salty raised her head and asked, "How will we get back to the Beacon of Hope Lighthouse to become lighthouse keepers?" Her voice held tears, mourning the loss of a dream.

"The glider is useless," said Schraeder.

"There you are. I've been looking for you two," said the Professor as he landed next to them.

"How are you, Professor?" asked the Navigator.

"Doing well. Good to see you again, too."

"Professor Watt. We've missed you." Salty and Schraeder said as they hugged him.

"Well, I've missed you too." The Professor wiped his glasses, squatted down and looked at them, eyeball to eyeball, and said, "Navigator, I think you've given me two excellent recruits to be lighthouse keepers. I'll meet you back at the Lighthouse."

Salty and Schraeder looked at each other, their mouths dropped open, their eyes bugged out, and their smiles became brighter than anyone had ever seen.

"Thank you so much," they said wholeheartedly as the Professor left.

Turning back to the Navigator, "We still don't know how we will get back to the Beacon of Hope Lighthouse," said Schraeder. "Remember, we destroyed the Professor's hang glider, but with you here, anything is possible. Will you help us?"

"Somebody need a ride?" A welcome voice from the past came from the beach. It was Brave-and-Faithful. He didn't look the same. He and his oars were completely healthy, like new. "Climb aboard when you're ready."

Seaworthy and Alby returned and were just as excited to see him as were Salty and Schraeder.

"Good to see you, Brave-and-Faithful," said Alby.

Seaworthy walked around, admiring his friend's wonderful new look. "Have you seen Fairhaven?" he asked, with great longing to hear about his friend.

"Ask him yourself," replied Brave-and-Faithful.

"Ahoy! Seaworthy, how are you, my friend?" It was Fairhaven. Seaworthy, with tears in his eyes, flew out to be with his friend.

"Oh, Fairhaven, I have missed you so much!" he cried.

"You look great, Seaworthy. You've matured a lot. The Navigator tells me you are growing up to be a fine young seagull."

"What's the Port of Heaven like?" he asked.

"It's everything the Navigator said. It's wonderful."

"Navigator," asked Schraeder, "what about Blanding? We really miss him."

"Hey, you two! I've missed you, too!"

"Look!" cried Salty, pointing off shore. "It's Blanding! Navigator, can we go out to him?"

"Please," begged Schraeder.

"Hop in," said Brave-and-Faithful. They scurried aboard and hitched a ride out to their old friend.

Climbing up the rope ladder, they paused and gave Blanding a kiss on his hull while shedding tears of joy. The Navigator watched from the shore and basked in the beautiful reunion.

"How did you get here? We thought you left us forever!" exclaimed Salty.

"The Navigator never gave up on me. After I left you with Fairhaven, I was thinking about all that had happened; I had to know if it was true. Would the Navigator give me a second chance to go to the Port of Heaven? My whole life I tried to do everything my way. It felt like I was carrying the weight of the whole world on my deck. I finally realized I couldn't make it on my own. I no longer knew what love and friendship felt like. I thought I was destined to be alone forever, but the Navigator changed all that. I am so grateful that he never gave up on me. Changes began happening the moment he stepped on board. Now here I am with you, my two good friends. I am so sorry for the way I treated you. Please forgive me."

"Of course we forgive you!" chorused Salty and Schraeder.

As they visited, Karl had lagged behind and sat on the beach, missing Chloe. He smiled when he thought of Brickwater's forgiveness and seeing Fairhaven's and Blanding's arrivals. As he sat on the beach, a shell washed up next to him. He picked it up, and remembered the Navigator's words to him to find the shell that had spoken to him. He picked it up slowly and cautiously brought it to his ear.

"You are loved."

He looked at the shell, returned it back to his ear and heard, "You are loved."

He was puzzled, for the words were not coming from the shell.

"You are loved!"

He heard it again. He looked down the beach and saw someone heading toward him. He jumped to his feet.

"Mom, Dad?" He spoke quietly, not sure what he was seeing. The closer they came, he recognized they were indeed his mom and dad.

"Mom, Dad!" he yelled, and ran faster to meet them.

"Karl!" they yelled out. "It's really him!" they said to each other through tears of joy as they ran to meet him.

His dad opened his wings to embrace him

From that moment on Crow never existed again. It was real. It was definitely not a dream; Karl was reunited with his parents.

The reunion continued with laughter and tears, hugs and kisses. It was an affection he had long forgotten ever existed.

"At last I know what love is! I love you, Mom and Dad."

"We love you too, and we've missed you terribly."

"How did you find me?"

A scent of roses rushed in with a sudden breeze.

Karl looked over his shoulder while still embracing his parents. He watched his family of friends and their wild antics of excitement celebrating Karl's joyous reunion.

As the family hugs began to let up, Karl turned to look at the sunset and saw Fairhaven and the Navigator sailing together, smiling and waving at him. It was the ending of a beautiful day, quite a turnaround from how the morning began. He realized the Navigator had been watching over him his whole life, never out of his sight.

Karl softly said, "He really loves me."

"Who loves you, honey?" His mom had overheard his words.

"The Navigator."

"Of course he does, he loves everyone."

A loud shout of joyous laughter was heard, followed by a stampede of friends rushing toward him with sand flying everywhere.

Seaworthy yelled out: "Group Hug!"

Alby, Seaworthy, Salty, Schraeder and Lovely descended on Karl while in the distance could be heard, "Come on, Walter, you're so slow sometimes!" It was Gwen beckoning, "Honey Babe, catch up."

Shelby was hanging on for dear life as Walter swayed to and fro, waddling as quickly as he could with Shelby clinging onto his ear.

"Oww! Not so hard, Shelby!"

"Not so fast, Walter!"

"Come on, you two!" scolded Gwen.

Walter and Shelby paused, looked at each other and sighed, then laughed. "Hang on!"

The group bowled over Karl, smooshing him to the ground with laughter. The planned hug turned into a huge pile-on.

Karl's parents quickly got out of the way, observed the rollicking fun, then his dad grabbed his mom and shouted, "Coming through!" They dove on top.

Gwen and Walter with Shelby finally caught up just as Karl's mom and dad were jumping onto the pile.

Seaworthy found himself eyeball to eyeball with Karl and wheezed, "I like Karl much better than Crow."

"Me too," said Karl, almost out of breath.

One by one they removed themselves from the pile.

"Mom, Dad. This is my family of friends." Karl proceeded to introduce everyone to his parents.

Later Karl sat down on the beach by himself, feeling overwhelmed by everything. He pulled up a blade of tall grass and began chewing on it, wishing Chloe could have been there for this moment. He knew she was safe with the Navigator and Fairhaven. He smiled, just thinking of her.

A wave splashed up and something nudged him. He chuckled, it was the familiar shell he had encountered so many times in recent days. He picked it up, wondering if it would speak to his heart one more time. He brushed off the wet sand and held it up to his ear.

"You are loved, forever in my heart you are loved." Karl's eyes filled with tears of joy and happiness, it was Chloe's voice.

Karl spoke into the shell while looking at the horizon: "And we were born to fly."

Be sure to pick up the authors first book *Fairhaven, Adventures on the sea called Life*. It is available at Amazon and most other on-line retailers.

www.ingramcontent.com/pod-product-compliance
Lightning Source LLC
Chambersburg PA
CBHW060421260626
47161CB00005B/1730